"I refused your invitation yesterday."

Donna lost her patience and rushed on, "And I'm refusing today. I have a great deal to do and—"

"You should have planned your day accordingly," Daniel interrupted.
"I did."

"I simply haven't got the time to lunch with you." Her eyes flicked past him, around her busy *pâtisserie*.

"Then make time."

"Now look—" She had been going to say something about making life easier for them both if he would just take no for an answer. But she never got that far.

Daniel merely sighed, as if bored, took hold of her and flung her over his shoulder. Donna heard the giggles of her customers and a male voice saying, "That's the way to handle 'em."

Then there was the noise of the traffic as Daniel stepped into the street with her and turned left....

Books by Claudia Jameson

HARLEQUIN PRESENTS

690—GENTLE PERSUASION
712—FOR PRACTICAL REASONS
737—DAWN OF A NEW DAY
777—THE FRENCHMAN'S KISS
817—THE SCORPIO MAN
867—ROSES, ALWAYS ROSES

HARLEQUIN ROMANCE

2523—LESSON IN LOVE
2565—THE MELTING HEART
2578—NEVER SAY NEVER
2594—YOURS...FAITHFULLY
2691—A TIME TO GROW

These books may be available at your local bookseller.

Don't miss any of our special offers. Write to us at the
following address for information on our newest releases.

Harlequin Reader Service
P.O. Box 52040, Phoenix, AZ 85072-2040
Canadian address: P.O. Box 2800, Postal Station A,
5170 Yonge St., Willowdale, Ont. M2N 6J3

CLAUDIA JAMESON

roses, always roses

Harlequin Books

TORONTO • NEW YORK • LONDON
AMSTERDAM • PARIS • SYDNEY • HAMBURG
STOCKHOLM • ATHENS • TOKYO • MILAN

With grateful thanks to Annette and to Dennis

Harlequin Presents first edition March 1986
ISBN 0-373-10867-2

Original hardcover edition published in 1985
by Mills & Boon Limited

CHAPTER ONE

TREMBLING, shaken, Donna Kent inched her way slowly into the parking space beside the Mini and the Transit van in the yard at the back of her shop. It was a tight squeeze, though she did appreciate her luck in having a private parking spot in the heart of Richmond. It wasn't the awkwardness of parking that was making her hands tremble, it was the way she had been plunged into the past only five minutes ago by Daniel Conrad's doppelgänger. She had glimpsed the man only briefly as he pulled up beside her at the traffic lights on her way into town, and by the time she registered why his face was so familiar he had turned left at the filter light, leaving Donna to stare after the bulky black Volvo as if it were being driven by a ghost.

Of course it hadn't actually been Daniel Conrad, just someone who looked like him. Or rather, someone who looked as he had looked six years ago. The bastard had probably changed during the past six years. Who didn't change in that length of time? Besides, what would he be doing in Surrey when his business, his home, his wife and all his relatives were in Lincolnshire? She asked this of herself because some ten days earlier something similar had happened. She had been driving the van on that occasion, just north of Surbiton, but the look-alike had been on foot, had crossed the road some two hundred yards in front of her and, excellent though her eyesight was, she had not been able to see his features at that distance. But there had been something, just *something* about the man, that had reminded her of Daniel Conrad.

Donna had dismissed the incident then as she dismissed it from her mind now. She had other things to think about, plenty of them. She got out of her emerald green Spitfire, taking care not to bang the door against Siggy's mini-van, and told herself that if he ever changed it for something bigger, parking would become impossible.

Glancing at her watch, she headed not for the back door of the shop but for the bank. It was nine twenty-five and it was pay-day. Every Friday she went to the bank and collected the necessary cash with which to make up the wages of those employees who preferred to be paid that way. She had been working at home, typing customers' accounts, ploughing through P.A.Y.E. tables then writing pay-slips, since seven that morning. It was always the same on a Friday; it was a hard day and it wouldn't end till around midnight. But that didn't matter. Donna Kent thrived on hard work.

After leaving the bank, she walked briskly through the morning sunshine to her place of business, the shop which had once been called 'Gee's Pâtisserie'. It was still a pâtisserie but the sign over the window now read: 'Kent Catering Services', and that sign had been put up four years ago, when Donna was twenty. She had done well in those four years. She had done very well in the past *six* years, considering how green, how naïve, she had been at eighteen. And considering how her world had come apart, how shattered she had been by her father's suicide. She thought again of the vision in the Volvo, the man who had reminded her so vividly of . . . No, it *couldn't* have been him. It was merely her hatred of Daniel Conrad that was making her over-react. But she didn't blame herself for doing so, she thought no less of herself because she'd been so shaken, because her hands had started trembling. After all, who wouldn't be enraged by the sight of the man who had been largely responsible for her father's destruction?

The front door of the shop was open and the smell of Siggy's home-made bread wafted on to the street. Already there was a queue for it. On Fridays and Saturdays there was always a queue for Siggy's goodies—the fresh cream cakes he made to his own recipes, the pies sweet and savoury, the quiches, pastries, pasties, the rolls, the loaves—they would all be gone before noon, leaving for sale only those items they bought from manufacturers and big bakeries.

With a smile, a nod and a 'Good morning' to assistants and customers, Donna made her way through the shop. She bypassed the kitchen and went directly to her office. This was a tiny room but it served its purpose. In the confined space there was all she really needed to run her catering business, a filing cabinet, two chairs, a desk and a telephone. Two more filing cabinets, another desk, a typewriter, staff and customers' files were kept at home in her two bedroomed house. Well, her one bedroom, one office, house!

Glancing again at her watch, she dumped her briefcase and her shoulder-bag on the desk. It was ten to ten. Any minute now Siggy would come in and start flapping about the preparations for tonight's party. Kent Catering Services were supplying all the food, and five dozen champagne glasses, for a twenty-first birthday party over in Twickenham that evening and, while this was not an unusual job for them, it was enough to send Siggy into a panic. Having panicked and moaned and insisted there wasn't enough time in which to do everything *perfectly,* he would then go up the two flights of stairs leading to the attic which was his bedroom. In there he would sit, in some unimaginable yogic knot, for an hour, 'meditating and soothing his spirit', after which he would take a regular nap for an hour. And nothing, but *nothing,* would deter Siggy from this two-hour daily ritual. Still, he was entitled. He started work every day, six days a week, at six in the morning.

Donna smiled to herself. Perhaps it was this ritual of meditation and rest that kept Siggy sane, speaking loosely, tongue-in-cheek. He was certainly the most eccentric man she had ever met. He was both predictable and unpredictable, an artist in his own right, a darling and something of a wizard to boot. In short, he was her friend and her most valued, and valuable, employee.

'Morning, Donna, love.'

'Good morning, Siggy.'

At ten on the dot Siegfried Gee came into the office, an unlit cigarette dangling between his lips. He sank into a chair and fished around for his lighter. 'How the hell are we going to get through this afternoon's lot? I mean, who ever heard of a twenty-first birthday party starting at seven in the evening? It's not civilised. Besides, they probably won't eat till ten or eleven so they should've chosen a different menu. I can't guarantee making decent soufflés at nine o'clock at night, especially in an electric oven.' He snorted. His hands were waving about and his voice was raised slightly. 'I don't like these half-hot, half-cold affairs, they're more trouble than they're worth.'

Donna smiled at him. When he was predictable, he was a comfort to her. His shortened name was appropriate in more ways than one. Siggy. For when he was not in the kitchen, he was smoking. Constantly. But he never, ever, smoked in the kitchen. Nor was anyone else allowed to. And he never seemed to get his overalls stained, unlike anyone else. Underneath his pristine, white, chef's jacket he was dressed in washed-out blue denim, always, and beneath his beloved, tall white hat, he was as blond as Donna herself. The difference was that her hair was as straight as a die whilst Siggy's was a mass of curls, though he didn't pretend they were natural, he had his hair permed regularly. 'They're not more trouble than they're worth, Siggy. Customers pay for the trouble—we make a nice profit.'

'You,' Siggy corrected, 'make a nice profit.'

Kent Catering Services were imaginative and flexible. If a customer wanted a cold buffet *and* soufflés for sixty people, that's what he got. And that's what he paid for. Whether it was for an office luncheon for customers, a staff party or merely a sandwich for the company's Chairman, KCS were equal to it. If they were required to do all the cooking in the kitchen of a private house, for a dinner party of two or twenty, or supply a five tier cake and all that went with it for a wedding, birthday, a christening, whatever, they were up to it. And KCS did the job superlatively well. There were never any complaints. Their diary was filled months ahead, with very few gaps. All this, the customers paid for. All this had taken a great deal of dedication and hard work on the party of Donna and Siggy ... and a lot of patience over the years while their reputation had been growing.

Donna frowned now. Siggy's remark had given her the perfect cue. She wanted to talk to him, again, about her plans to form a limited company. She had already mentioned this once to him, only to have him wave the topic away with a shrug of uninterest. But she didn't want him to be uninterested; Siggy put almost as many hours into the business as she did. She wanted him to be her partner, not her employee. It was only right and fair.

But Siggy Gee was a strange character. As a customer of his pâtisserie, she had got to know him four years ago when she had been looking for shop premises to rent. At that time, Donna had been working in the staff canteen of a large department store and had been running a catering service, in a very small way, in her spare time, mainly baking cakes for people. Siggy had told her that he was looking for someone to take over his lease on the shop and the accommodation that went with it, reasoning that he couldn't get rid of one without the other. The top and bottom of it was, and he made no effort to hide the fact, that Siggy's business was running at a loss. He was, simply, hopeless with costing, hopeless with money, the preservation of it and the spending of it. Though he had at that time been in the shop for sixteen months and was doing a roaring trade, he was not making a living. And that, bless him, was all Siggy wanted from life. A living. A guaranteed, fixed sum of money every month. Peace of mind. No responsibility of a financial nature.

So Donna had taken over the lease and the business, and Siggy still lived on the premises. What had once been his bedroom on the first floor was now a stockroom. His bathroom and small sitting room were still intact—and never trespassed upon by Donna—and the attic had been converted into a place where he could sleep. Donna had not wanted or needed the accommodation, only the space, the kitchens, an office and/or a shop front, an address in town. She had not wanted the pâtisserie as such—though it, too, made a profit these days, now she was in charge.

Her relationship with Siggy was a curious one and a very special one. Their unspoken understanding of one another prohibited any questions of too personal a nature. Siggy knew only a little about her parents, where she came from, what her culinary training had been. This, plus the fact that she owned a house, a big house, in the Lincolnshire Wolds. He knew that this was her inheritance from her parents, that she rented it out to people, but he did not know that it was her *only* inheritance from a father who had been very comfortably off, once. Nor did he know the circumstances surrounding her father's death, he didn't know that Joseph Kent had committed suicide. Donna knew it, but her father's death had never been proved as suicide. There simply hadn't been any evidence that his death was other than accidental.

Likewise, Siggy's personality and character aside, Donna knew very little about him. Born of an Austrian mother and an English father, he had spent the first twenty years of his life in Austria. After that he had travelled almost world-wide; he had worked in the kitchens of umpteen hotels, top-class hotels, and had qualified, had become what he was today—a superb cook and the finest of pastry chefs, a man of great flair and imagination.

He was, he claimed, now forty. There again, he could

have been forty-five because he had told her he was forty on his birthday last February, and the February before that ...! But none of this mattered to Donna. She knew only that she liked him enormously, that she trusted him totally and that these feelings were mutual. What Siggy did on Sundays and on the evenings he wasn't working with her was his business. She never asked him what he did in his spare time and he never volunteered the information. Nor did he question her motives for working so damned hard, or anything else.

She frowned at him now, feeling slightly guilty. 'Siggy, the only reason I'm getting the profit from this business is because you refused to enter into partnership with me. Now listen.' Her left hand came up, her fingers spread apart as she tried to reason with him. 'I've told you I'm about to form a limited company. Now don't panic. You can be a co-director. With me. And it's a——'

He did it again. One long, slender hand came out and he waved her words away, almost flinching. 'I'm not interested, love. You pay me well and that's all I want. You have the profit, you have the headaches. Just give me my monthly cheque, I'm happy.'

'But you work——'

'I do not, in case you haven't noticed, work myself into the ground. *You* work most nights, I don't. *You* don't take time off during the day, I do. *You* don't forget work on Sundays, I do. You pay the bills, you do the costings, you pander to the customers, you cope with them, I don't. You hire and organise the staff, you delegate, I don't. You do the books, the wages, I don't. I'm more than happy with our arrangement. I'm doing my thing in the kitchen and I'm making a living from it. What more could I ask? What more do I want from life, for God's sake?'

'I——' In truth, she didn't know how to answer. If that was all Siggy wanted, that was all he wanted. Maybe he was to be envied. He was not driven, as she was, by a need to prove something. To prove something to herself as well as to some other people.

There had been a time when Donna hadn't known the difference between a limited company and a non-limited company, a public company or a corporation and so forth. Nor had she, at the age of eighteen, known what the words 'probate' or 'creditors' meeting' or 'assets' meant, not exactly. She hadn't known, then, what auditors did, what the role of a liquidator was. Although her father had been a very successful business man he had never spoken to her about business matters, so his world and all these words had been alien to her.

At eighteen, while in the eyes of the law she was an adult, was eligible to vote, she had lived very much in a cocoon, a safe, secure world, a world which had splintered into nothingness when her father went bankrupt and, very shortly afterwards, died.

Now, she closed her eyes against the memory of all that, just briefly, just long enough to remind herself that she had everything under control these days; that she was no longer as green as the grass, no longer ignorant of the pitfalls and advantages of having one's own business. Nor was she unaware of the cunning and the devious farsightedness some businessmen could sink to . . . especially those with the surname of Conrad.

She opened her eyes again to look at Siggy, thin, short, curly-headed Siggy with blue eyes several shades lighter than her own. Siggy with the inevitable cigarette in his mouth. 'But it wouldn't heap responsibility on your shoulders,' she assured him. 'You could have just a nominal share in the company. One share. I'll have ninety-nine and still be the boss. You see, Siggy, there has to be another director.'

'Then ask Una,' he said, referring to their most accomplished part-timer. 'But in any case, why,' he went on in his perfect but accented English, 'do you want to be a limited company? I know you need another director, but not me, love. No, I'm not even interested in having one share. I'm very, very happy with the status quo.'

'Being a limited company affords you some protection,' Donna explained, answering his question firstly. '*If* something goes wrong, *if* I mismanage and end up bankrupt, I wouldn't lose my house, for instance. To pay debts with, I mean. You see, my little house here will have nothing to do with the company. It's *mine*.'

Siggy looked at her blankly.

'It's safe. It will be safe, *mine*, if ever the business gets into hot water,' she went on limply. 'Don't you see? So would my house in Lincolnshire. There are advantages, there's some—some security in being a limited company. Siggy? Why are you looking at me like that?'

Siggy Gee was looking at her like that for several reasons. Anyone less likely to fail in business, he couldn't imagine. This woman was as solid and sound as a rock. To the point where it worried him. She was twenty-four years old going on sixty. He had never, ever, met anyone so single-minded, so bloody determined in all his life. There were times when he wanted to take hold of her by the throat and shake her till her brain rattled. And it was a good brain. If only it weren't so preoccupied with work, money, work, profit. What the hell was she trying to prove? And to whom?

Donna Kent was a tiny, blue-eyed blonde with a figure that made men turn in the street for a second look ... a third look. But she never noticed. Everything she wore, everything she did, was chosen and planned for maximum efficiency, practicality. But she never registered that, either. Her hair was the colour and texture of spun gold, and what did she do with it? She wore it with a boring fringe, with a boring parting down the centre, with a boring but practical elastic band at the nape. Out of the way. Tidy. Efficient.

It looked awful.

She dressed in all the varying colours of mud. Oh, her clothes were quality ones, our Donna never wore cheap stuff (false economy), but they were drab, drab, drab. It was not that she was mean, far from it, it was just that she didn't seem to notice that she had been born *female*, a gorgeous female at that. With deep blue eyes which got deeper when she got emotional or enthusiastic about something, which was always, only, business, in Siggy's experience, she could motivate you into giving one hundred and one per cent effort to her, for her, with a single gaze.

To put it simply, Siggy loved her.

And nobody regretted more than he that he couldn't love her in a different way. He wished he could love her as she deserved to be loved. He wished he could look after her, touch her, hold her, explain to her and make her see that it was wrong, wrong, wrong to work eighteen hours a day, day in and day out, no matter what this bee in her bonnet was.

But he couldn't.

He could only love her detachedly, asking no questions because he had no right to, do his best for her and be grateful to her. And, yes, be a little in awe of her in some ways. He had never seen her lose her temper, had never even seen her cross or rattled. Nor had he known her to be faced with a problem with which she couldn't cope. She was, as the Americans might put it, very laid back, a cool blonde English woman who knew exactly where she was going.

The wildest thing about this woman, the only thing that didn't fit in with what he knew of her, was her sports car and its emerald-green colour. It seemed, to him, some sort of giveaway, so out of character that he couldn't help wondering what she was really like, deep down inside. The real Donna Kent. What was she? Who was she?

He smiled at her as she sighed, opening her briefcase to extract wads of money for the wages. 'I'm going upstairs, love. See you later.'

Donna nodded. Once the wages were finished, she had several joints of meat to roast and a hundred vol-au-vents to create. Siggy would do the rest later and, at six on the dot, they would load the Transit van with their goodies, and the champagne glasses from the stockroom, and head together for Twickenham.

It was a typical Friday.

Saturday would be as hectic. She didn't need to look in the diary to be reminded that Kieren Gardner's barbecue was taking place in the gardens of his home tomorrow night. It was to be a private-cum-business affair, for clients who were also friends.

Kieren Gardner had asked Donna out several times and she was expert at dodging him without offending him. He was handsome and in his thirties, a partner in Messrs Douglas, Gardner and Fairchild, solicitors and commissioners of oaths. He was a good customer; he called upon the services of KCS both for luncheons or parties in his offices and for private functions at his home, the latter less frequently but some two or three times a year.

She carried on stuffing money into envelopes. It was time to delegate again, she realised that. She had to get someone to keep the books and do the wages. She knew she was working to maximum capacity and had been for quite some time. Her aching back told her that often these days. If she were going to be equal to the demands of her ever-increasing list of clients, she personally had to devote most of her time to that which she did best of all: dealing with enquiries, visiting prospective customers, costing the jobs and quoting, organising and overseeing the staff. The time when she spent her entire day in the kitchen had gone, which in some ways was rather a pity because she loved cooking. Nowadays she did the planning and left most, but not yet all, of the kitchen work, the cooking and baking, to Siggy and the others.

She had come a long way since leaving Lincolnshire but she still had a long way to go. She was doing very well but it wasn't enough. She was earning a comfortable living but she was by no means rich, not rich in the way her father had once been rich.

But she had plans.

One day she would go back to live in Lincolnshire. To live in what had been her parents' house, the beautiful house which had been her inheritance, the only thing her father had left her after his death. Thanks to Daniel Conrad, that's all her father had been able to bequeath her.

In the final analysis Donna had to admit that so much pride was involved in all this. Pride was her motivation, not money for money's sake. One day, she was going back to live in her childhood home. This was her dream, that which motivated her. One day she was going back to face all the villagers who had done all that gossiping . . . and she would hold her head very high while showing them *all* what she, Joseph Kent's daughter, was made of.

Early on Saturday morning, she woke up with a slight headache. It was nothing new. She ignored it; it was only due to shortage of sleep, it would wear off.

Bleary-eyed, she padded from her bedroom to her bathroom and took a shower, brushed her teeth and applied the minimum of make-up. By then she was in second gear. She made her bed, hung up her dressing gown and nightie and pulled on a pair of thirty denier tights, a crisp white blouse and a grey suit.

The afternoon found her working in top gear with Siggy and Una in the kitchen at the shop. At six in the evening, Pauline and Margaret Nash came trooping through the back door, complaining about the midsummer heat and saying they were glad tonight's job was outdoors. Pauline and Margaret were sisters, both students and casual waitresses. They, Donna and Siggy would cope with Kieren Gardner's barbecue that evening. Donna and Siggy would cook, the girls would keep the guests' plates and glasses filled.

'You missed a good one last night, girls,' Siggy told them laughingly. 'That twenty-first in Twickers. Pity you weren't on duty, you'd have had a good laugh. A real boozy do, wasn't it, Donna?'

Donna grunted, not looking up from the task in hand. She was carefully counting steaks and sausages as she piled them into a cold box. Last night's party had not amused her. She didn't understand why some people thought they weren't having fun unless they were utterly smashed. Thinking of which, eleven of her best champagne glasses had been broken. The cost of the breakages would, of course, be added to the customer's bill.

She picked up a spare copy of the worksheet for that night and handed it to Pauline. 'Tablecloths, glasses, our uniforms, cutlery as listed, would you load these into the van, Pauline? Oh, and put in an extra dozen plates. Mr Gardner always asks last minute guests he forgets to tell us about.'

It was Siggy's turn to grunt. 'Mr Gardner,' he muttered, 'is a pain in the bum.'

'Kieren Gardner,' Donna amended, 'is a very nice man and a very good customer.' But she wasn't actually thinking about how nice Kieren was. She was irked by thoughts of the extra business she could have been doing in catering for his party, if she had more storage space, if she had bigger premises. As things stood, she was unable to hire out tables and chairs for functions such as this one, and the barbecue equipment, and consequently Kieren had had to spend money elsewhere in order to get the extra garden furniture and things he needed. Now, if she had bigger premises and more storage space . . .

On the drive to Kieren's house, at the wheel of the Transit van, while Siggy followed in the Mini van, Donna thought about the formation of her limited company and the way she could expand her business. The chatter of Pauline and Margaret went over her head while she plotted and planned.

Once at Kieren's house, however, she began to concentrate fully on the job in hand. It was seven o'clock; his guests were due to start arriving at eight-thirty.

By eight o'clock, all the preparations were done and Siggy was slouching against a tree in the garden, smoking his last few cigarettes before he started cooking. Pauline and Margaret were checking tables and cutlery, a gardener was fiddling with lights in the trees, and inside the house the hired disc jockey was setting up his equipment and sifting through his records.

All was quiet for the moment. The evening was hot and beautifully clear, the scene was set. Donna and her staff were organised and waiting, dressed in their immaculate navy and white striped pinafores and caps.

'Donna?' Kieren came up to her, his eyes flicking over her appreciatively but a little worriedly. 'Are you okay? You look pretty washed-out.' He slipped an arm around her shoulders, smiling down at her. 'But pretty is the operative word. You work too hard, do you know that?'

'So you keep telling me.'

'Come inside and have a drink. I'd like you to meet my sister and brother-in-law, they're down from Scotland for the weekend. You haven't met them before, have you?'

She shook her head and followed him through the wide French windows which led into the drawing room. She liked Kieren well enough but she wished he would cut out the flirting and keep their relationship on a strictly business footing. He might fancy her but she didn't fancy him—tall, dark and handsome though he was. And he was clever, successful. The law practice in which he was a partner had several branches including one in Lincoln's Inn, London, at which his father worked.

Mr Gardner senior was in the drawing room now. She shook hands with him and exchanged pleasantries. He lived in the centre of London and had asked her in the past to cater for a couple of functions for him, but Donna had turned the jobs down. She didn't work in inner London, there was too much competition and it wasn't worth the hassle of ploughing through the traffic. In any case, she wasn't short of work in the areas she did service.

For the next five minutes, the few people present drank and chatted and it was only when Kieren said something about his houseguest that Donna felt a flash of unease.

'Where's Daniel?' he asked of his sister, who said she had no idea. 'He's probably still in his room, working,' he muttered. Sighing, shaking his head, he turned to Donna. 'My houseguest,' he explained. 'He was supposed to be down here at eight sharp but he's probably still poring over papers. Like you, Donna, Daniel is a workaholic. Will you excuse me a moment?'

It was the name Daniel that made her feel uneasy, which was ridiculous. Kieren's houseguest was no doubt another solicitor, one who pored over papers when he was supposed to be attending a party. There was, she told herself, more than one man named Daniel in the country.

'I'm sorry, Sally, what did you say?' She hadn't heard a word Kieren's sister had just said to her.

The other girl laughed. 'I was asking you when do you get time off? I mean, you don't work every night, do you? Surely your staff can . . .'

That was all Donna heard. Oblivious to how rude she must seem to her customer's sister, oblivious to the way Kieren smiled at her as he came back into the room with his errant houseguest, Donna could do no more than stare at the newcomer.

It was the man she had seen in the Volvo.

No, he hadn't been merely a look-alike, he hadn't been a mirage. He had been, he *was*, Daniel Conrad.

And he was here. In the same room with her. Looking exactly as he had looked when last she had seen him, six years earlier.

Intimidatingly tall and broad, he was looking at Donna as he and Kieren walked towards her. His eyes were narrowed slightly as he tried to put her name to her face . . . then realisation dawned in them.

He stared at her.

And she stared at him.

CHAPTER TWO

DONNA went rigid, she could feel the blood draining from her face. When Kieren began to make introductions, she wasn't able to stop him, to tell him it was unnecessary. All she wanted to do was to spit in Daniel Conrad's face and get *out* of his sight, get away from him just as she had in the past.

It was he who stopped Kieren. 'Miss Kent and I have met,' he said, his eyes not leaving hers for an instant.

She heard rather than saw Kieren's surprise. 'Really? How? When?' But he didn't expect an answer, it seemed. He just went prattling on. 'Dan and I have known each other for years. We were up at Oxford at the same time.'

Nobody responded. Donna hadn't even heard properly. There was a film of perspiration on her forehead, on the palms of her hands. It was as though her loathing of Daniel Conrad were seeping out of her. He was regarding her with interest, as if curious to see what she would say, how she would react.

She reacted in the only way she could, given the circumstances. She excused herself and went upstairs. She locked herself in a bathroom and sat on the lid of the lavatory, her hands clamped tightly against her now burning face. Against her closed eyelids she could still see the picture of the man downstairs. Good-looking, big, blond and brawny, the vision of him sickened her. Daniel Conrad, well-groomed, as ever, neatly dressed, as ever. With that deep, educated voice of his and eyes that were deceptively gentle, he had all the appearance of a well-bred English gentleman. But Donna knew otherwise.

He was as devious and as ruthless as they came.

Shaking with anger, she tried very, very hard to pull

22

herself together, to get control of herself. Her mind refused to comply, it was zipping back through the years, to the time when she was eighteen and a student at the catering college, where she boarded in Eastbourne.

It had been just a week before the Easter holidays began when Donna was summoned to the college Principal's office.

She was seeing herself as she had been as she stood in that office, hearing the woman's voice urging her to sit down. She had sat, alarmed at the Principal's tone, at the look on her face. 'What is it, Mrs Webster?'

'Donna ... I've just had a telephone call ... I'm afraid I have very bad news for you ...'

Then Donna was no longer seeing herself detachedly, suddenly it was as if she were really *there*, in that office again, inside herself and feeling precisely as she had felt on being told that her father had died two hours ago in a road accident. Numb, disbelieving, empty, confused. The details of the accident hadn't made sense at the time. Donna's father had been alone in his car, driving from his home in the Lincolnshire Wolds on the A46, in the direction of Lincoln. He had died instantaneously when his car suddenly veered off the highway into the solid concrete support of a bridge.

From the Principal's office Donna had telephoned her mother's elder sister who lived in Rotherham, then she immediately made her way home by train.

Her mother's sister, Elizabeth, and her husband Desmond were already at the house when she got there. This childless couple were Donna's only remaining relatives and though they hadn't got on terribly well with Joseph Kent, they were distraught.

Donna didn't weep, not for a long time. She was held and comforted by her aunt but she felt nothing, no emotion whatever. 'My poor darling,' her aunt crooned. 'This, when you lost your poor mother only eighteen months ago! I know how you're feeling, Donna, really I do. Poor child ...'

But Donna wasn't feeling anything.

Days passed, days that were hazy and unreal to Donna. They came and went, as did visitors to the house, people her aunt and uncle dealt with, as they dealt with the funeral arrangements. Joseph's funeral was well attended by people with faces both familiar and unfamiliar to his daughter.

She ate when she was urged to, she slept when she was able. It was March and one thing she did remember clearly about that awful time was that it rained day after day after day. She remembered also the day Uncle Desmond left for Rotherham. He was very apologetic, explaining that he had to get back to his job. But Aunt Elizabeth stayed on to look after her.

Joseph Kent's accident had appeared in the national press in one of those tiny, two-inch columns it was all too easy to miss. On the day the story was printed in the local paper, however, an entire page was used for the report, for the rehash of the details of the accident, witnesses' accounts ... and the fact that Joseph Kent had been declared bankrupt just a few weeks before his death.

That was the day when Donna's numbness lifted. That was the day the pain set in. And the indescribable anger.

She had had no idea about her father's bankruptcy. She had been at the catering college, hundreds of miles away, for the best part of a year. Joseph had told her nothing about the state of his business, he never had. He had been a builder, a very successful one—or so she'd thought.

Well-intentioned and trying to protect her, her aunt and uncle had not told her about her father's bankruptcy. They had spoken with his accountants and his solicitor, they had talked to the police about the accident, but they had not said anything to the press. The press—well, the local press simply found out, the way they do, and their exposé was pretty thorough.

On the day the article appeared, Donna's aunt

knocked on her bedroom door early in the morning. She broke the news to her niece then, realising she had to be told now, before she saw it in the paper.

'But I don't understand! I don't understand . . .' Over and over Donna said this. Her father, *bankrupt*? It wasn't possible! But before the day was out she understood a great many things.

Without making an appointment, without telling Elizabeth, Donna slipped out of the house and drove her aunt's car into Louth, where the offices of her father's accountants were. There, she demanded to see Mr Crompton, whom she'd met in the past when he had been at the house, talking business with her father.

A middle-aged man with thinning grey hair, Mr Crompton was acutely and obviously embarrassed. He had seen the newspaper. He knew more than the press had discovered. Considerably more. 'My dear . . . do sit down.'

Woodenly, Donna sat facing him, bemused, staring at him expectantly.

'I—er—you haven't spoken to your father's solicitor yet, I take it? I mean, you personally?' Mr Crompton's fingers were thrumming nervously, irritatingly, on his desk.

'Not yet. I want you to explain it to me. How can my father have gone bankrupt? What went wrong? I just can't believe this!'

'Donna, I'm afraid you're going to find—well, that there's no money. The house is safe, of course. Fortunately, it was never charged to the bank.'

'*Money?*' Incredulous, she couldn't stop staring at the man. 'I don't care about money! I've come here for an explanation.'

He didn't meet her eyes. 'Would you like a nice cup of tea, perhaps?'

'No, I would not! I want an explanation. I want to know what had happened to my father lately. What happened to his business? Why did he go bankrupt? How did it happen? And what does that mean, 'charged to the bank'? And what do you mean by saying that my home is safe? Daddy had lots of properties dotted around this shire.'

It was a long and painful interview, painful for both of them, and throughout it all Donna had the feeling that her father's accountant knew more than he was saying.

She asked a dozen questions of him and he answered them all but initially she remained in the dark, not understanding the words and phrases he used. 'Mr Crompton,' she said at length, 'could you just explain it all to me simply?'

'I'll try, Donna,' he said kindly, then proceeded to sit in silence for what seemed like an eternity. 'I—er—the first thing you must understand is that this kind of thing doesn't happen overnight. Joseph had made some bad decisions over the past year or so, he also had some bad luck, genuine bad luck. To be honest, he hadn't coped properly since the day your mother died.'

Donna looked down at her hands. She knew that much. She had still been living at home after her mother's death and she knew full well how affected her father had been by it. Alice Kent had never been a fit woman. For years her health had been delicate. She had had a heart malfunction since birth and indeed had been advised not to have any children. Of recent years, with new and advanced techniques, they could have operated with a good chance of improving her health. But Alice had refused to have the operation, just as she had insisted on having a child—just the one.

'My dear, the crux of the matter is that your father's creditors, his suppliers, wouldn't give him any more time in which to pay his debts. His main suppliers were Conrads, over in Lincoln. Joseph bought all his timber and his general supplies from them, as you probably know. He had been a customer of theirs for the past fifteen years, to my knowledge.'

'Why didn't they trust him? Why didn't they give him more time to pay?'

'Because there are limits,' came the gentle reply. 'Conrads are a big company but there are limits as to how many debts any business can stand. Your father owed them thousands, Donna, thousands.

'Now, some fifteen months ago he made an unfortunate speculation on a small office block here in Louth. By speculation, I mean that he didn't have a prospective buyer or prospective tenants for the place. It was an investment. He knew he would sell it or let it. Anyhow, his initial exploration of the ground, the site, was satisfactory but when building started he encountered problems. The ground wasn't as stable, as suitable, as he'd first thought. I won't blind you with science—this is not my field in any case—suffice it to say that Joseph had already sunk so much money into the building when suddenly he found himself having to put supports and God knows what else into the foundations. In short, he had to spend thousands more than he'd expected to spend.

'He borrowed from his bank. Banks, as you surely know, don't lend money on the strength of promises. To get the necessary cash he had to charge to the bank some of his other properties—namely that row of five terraced houses he had near Cabourne. The office building is still unfinished.

'In the meantime, the bungalows he was building on the Market Rasen site got held up because of the very bad winter we had. Timber supplies got ruined, there were various thefts from the site and at some point or another his employees were off sick, thanks to the 'flu epidemic, or they wouldn't or couldn't work because of the snow, all of which resulted in the delay in completion, the sale, of the properties. In turn, this meant that your father had no money coming in, no turnover of capital. Do you understand so far?'

Donna nodded dumbly. Mr Crompton's explanation went on and on. He did his best to paint fully for her the picture of her father's business life for about the past two years, clearly feeling ill at ease while he did so.

'. . . and the timing of all this was very unfortunate. These things happen, my dear. Especially to builders. Did you know that about one in five builders goes bankrupt?' he asked, as though this would make her feel better.

She said nothing. Her mind was boggling with it all. Worse, she still had the suspicion that the accountant knew something else, something about her father that he didn't want her to discover.

While outwardly she kept her composure, inwardly she was weeping. She had adored her father, had been so close to him; why hadn't he confided in her? Shared his troubles with her?

Of course the answer to that was obvious; she hadn't been around, she'd been away at college for months. The college was expensive, too, a fee-paying establishment which trained people very thoroughly in the culinary arts, in housecraft and needlework and other skills. But Joseph had never said a word about the fees, he had paid them term by term, and she had one more term to go, after Easter. That was paid for, too.

'. . . a question of who was going to start the procedure.'

'What?'

'The liquidation.'

'You've lost me. I'm sorry, I—I missed what you just said.'

'I was explaining . . . I was about to explain the steps, the procedure when . . .' Mr Crompton cleared his throat and shifted uneasily in his seat. 'When someone goes bankrupt.'

Donna lifted her head a little and took a deep breath. 'You've been very kind, Mr Crompton. I understand it all now. The house is mine, and all its contents. It's safe. But there's nothing else, no money. None at all.' She was about to get up but there was just one more thing she wanted to say, to say in defence of her father. 'You were right in saying that Daddy hadn't been the same man since my mother died. And there was her ill health for some years before that. Even though . . .' She broke off, swallowing against the lump in her throat. 'And even though we knew she wouldn't live to a grand old age, her death was still an awful shock, so I think . . . I think that in a way, Daddy sort of gave up. He—he did mismanage and he did have bad luck, but it wasn't his fault. He must have decided it was for the best, to go bankrupt.'

Mr Crompton looked at her in puzzlement for several seconds. 'For the best? Donna, your father didn't *decide* to go bankrupt. He did not go into voluntary liquidation.'

'What? I don't know what you mean, I don't really understand what liquidation means,' she admitted.

With a pained expression, Mr Crompton did his best to enlighten her. 'Joseph owed what amounts to a great deal of money to his creditors. That is to say, putting them all together, his debts were enormous. One of his suppliers called a creditors' meeting. At that meeting, it was decided to set the ball rolling with a view to having your father declared bankrupt. And this is what happened. In court. He was adjudged bankrupt. At that stage——'

'Did the bank do it?' she demanded. 'Was it their idea? Did they call the creditors' meeting?'

'No,' Mr Crompton said patiently. 'I've just explained to you that his debt to the bank wasn't all that significant. I told you he'd sold off certain assets in order to reduce his overdraft, and he'd charged his——'

'But . . . but . . .' Overwhelmed, unable to believe that someone had actually *done* this to her father, had forced him into bankruptcy, she stammered her confusion. 'B-but I—I thought—God in heaven! So Daddy hadn't given up, he was *forced* into this! Oh, I'll bet he was so *ashamed*! He must have felt like a failure. You didn't know him like I did, Mr Crompton, he was a very proud man, a self-made man who was proud of his achievements. Why, this is *awful*!'

Silence reigned for long, awkward moments.

'*Who* did it? Whose idea was it to gang up on my father?'

The accountant shrugged. 'Conrads, of course. They had cut off his supplies long since, which in turn added to the difficulties of——'

'*Conrads?*' Donna was on her feet now, more confused than ever. 'But Richard Conrad was Daddy's friend! Daddy—both my parents used to go to their home occasionally, for a drink or for dinner. I've met Mr Conrad several times. He's nice, he wouldn't do this——'

'I'm afraid he did. And you can't blame him, Donna.' He pressed his intercom and asked his secretary to bring in two cups of tea. He felt embarrassed and extremely sorry for Joseph's daughter. He couldn't tell her the rest of it, he simply couldn't. Besides, he didn't know for certain. He didn't actually *know*. He had only his suspicions. His relationship with Joseph Kent had been almost exclusively one of business, not a social one. His daughter was right; he hadn't known the man very well.

'And what good will it do them?' Donna was shouting now. 'Conrads? You can't get blood out of a stone! You can't get money from a man who hasn't got any!'

'They'll get some,' Mr Crompton said quietly. 'Your father's books are being examined right now. If I can just explain—the court appointed a liquidator. It's his job to take stock, as it were, then sell off the company assets, the properties your father's company owned, finished or unfinished, then the monies are divided between the creditors and they all end up with—whatever. So much in the pound.'

Donna sank back into her chair. She had gone so pale that the accountant was quite worried, he searched frantically for something to say to comfort her. He was very clumsy about it. 'I—er—they won't recoup all their money. My dear, I'm sure your father would have—Donna?'

She was sitting like a statue, motionless. Then she

nodded almost imperceptibly and tears streaked down her face. 'I see,' she whispered. 'I see. This explains it, doesn't it? The mystery of Daddy being in perfect health, that's what the autopsy showed, that he hadn't taken ill or something while driving. And the mystery of his car being in perfect working order. That's what the police said, that there was no apparent reason for the accident. It *wasn't* an accident!' she shouted suddenly. *'My father committed suicide!'*

The secretary came in at that instant, looking horrified at what she had heard. Donna shot to her feet and pushed past her, almost knocking the tea tray from her hands.

Mr Crompton caught up with her in the corridor outside. 'Donna! Miss Kent, please! Wait!'

She spun round to face him, breathless with anger and hurt. 'It's all right, Mr Crompton. You couldn't voice your suspicions, I see that. But you know as well as I do that Daddy killed himself, that it was no accident! I'm probably the last person to realise it! I'll bet everyone else knows it!'

'No! No, I don't know any such thing! Please wait, don't dash off like this, come and sit down and——'

'Let go of me! I've got business to attend to.'

'Business? What business?'

Wrenching her arm from his grasp, she shouted loudly enough for everyone in the building to hear. 'What business? I'm going to talk to my father's *murderer*, that's what! Richard Conrad. He killed Daddy just as surely as if he'd put a gun to his head. For money. Your money or your life. That's it!'

Mr Crompton let her go simply because he didn't know what else to do with her. She was hysterical, like a wildcat. He went back into his office, put his head in his hands and wondered what to do. By the time he had finished his tea, he had decided on the most sensible course. He picked up the telephone and dialled Conrads in Lincoln. He knew Richard Conrad wasn't around but with luck his son, Daniel, would be there. And Mr

Crompton felt it right that he should be told about the visitor who was probably on her way right now.

Donna was on her way. She was almost blind with fury. For days she had lived in a vacuum, for years she had lived in a cocoon. Yes, that was right. She had been protected from the realities of the big bad world all her life. She had been dearly loved and doted upon by her parents, had been their beloved and only child. Until she had left for college the previous year, she had never been away from home except for holidays. With her parents. They had always been there, supportive, spoiling her, looking after her.

She drove her aunt's car recklessly in the direction of Lincoln, feeling as if she were ageing as every minute passed. She was changing rapidly; she could actually feel it happening to her. Her existence hitherto had not prepared her for life's harsh realities. Nor had she been in any way prepared for her father's death. She had no idea how she was going to cope now, no idea what she was going to do, she no longer had any idea about her future. Her dreams of one day owning her own restaurant, dreams her father had encouraged every inch of the way, had gone up in smoke.

It hurt, it *hurt* that he had taken his own life. All right, he had lost his wife and then his business but was she, his daughter, not enough for him to live for? Obviously not.

'Damn you, Richard Conrad. Damn you *and* your son. Damn you to *hell*!'

She meant every word of it. She sped along the road on which her father had committed suicide and chanted these words over and over. They must both have been in on it, Richard and Daniel Conrad. She had never met Daniel but she knew he'd joined his father's company some years earlier.

So frustrated was she, so blinded by anger and hurt, it was some time before she realised that she didn't know exactly where she was going. She had to get out of the car on the outskirts of the town and look in a telephone

directory for the address of Conrads' works. She
discovered that they were east of Lincoln, about three
miles outside the town.

She found the place easily enough. She walked
through a massive yard in which three of the firm's
lorries were parked and wood-cutting machinery was
whirring noisily, into the building at the back. Finding
herself in some sort of warehouse in which umpteen
bathroom suites were on display, she yelled out to catch
someone's attention.

A man in brown overalls came scurrying towards her.
'I'm looking for Mr Conrad,' she told him. 'Where can
I find him?'

'You're looking for Mr Conrad?' he repeated
blankly, stupidly as far as Donna was concerned. 'Oh,
you must mean Mr Daniel!'

'No, I don't. I want to see Richard Conrad and I
want to see him *now*.'

'But, miss ... Mr Richard is in hospital. He's been
there for some time. His ulcer——'

Donna glared at the man. She wasn't interested in
what 'Mr Richard's' ulcer was doing. 'Then Daniel
Conrad will do. Where can I find him?'

'Well, the offices are upstairs, but perhaps——'

She didn't need to ask the question, she followed the
movement of his eyes and spotted the staircase. There
were more stockrooms on the first floor, unmanned,
and more on the second. She discovered that the offices
were on the third floor.

Storming through a door marked 'Reception', Donna
came face to face with a young woman who jumped
visibly as the office door slammed back on its hinges.

'Can I help you?'

'No. You can't. I want to see Daniel Conrad and I
want to see him now.'

'Have you got an appointment?' The girl was
obviously stalling, obviously puzzled.

'No I haven't got a bloody appointment! Nor do I
need one. Just tell me where I can find Daniel Conrad.'

'Here, right here.'

Donna started at the sound of a deep, masculine voice coming from directly behind her. She spun round to face a broad-shouldered giant of a man who intimidated her not one iota. 'Are you Daniel Conrad?'

'I am.' He inclined his head slightly, unsmiling, unruffled, just as though he'd been expecting her. But he couldn't have been. 'And you are?'

'Donna Kent.' She spat out her surname. '*Kent*. Got it? I'm the daughter of the man who was a very good customer of yours for over fifteen years. I'm the daughter of the man who was buried recently, the man who was a friend of your father's. The man who committed suicide on the A46. Now do you remember? Kent, *Joseph Kent*.'

Still unruffled, unflinching, Daniel Conrad invited her into his office. 'If you'll just come into my office, Miss Kent, perhaps we can sort out——'

'No I won't!' she yelled. 'No, we can't. *We* can't sort out anything, Mr Conrad. We can't bring my father back. Neither you nor your father, with all your money and all your power, can bring my father back! He was a wonderful man, the very salt of this earth, but now he's dead, *dead!* And you killed him. Both of you!'

At that point Daniel turned and walked into his office, through a door on which his name and the words 'Financial Director' appeared. Obliged to follow him, Donna stalked into the room and slammed the door behind her. 'Why did you do it, Mr Conrad? You're not hard up for money. *Why* did you do it?'

'Sit down, Miss Kent.' He sat, so calm and collected that Donna wanted to hit him.

'No! Just answer my question.'

'I—we didn't cause your father's death, Miss Kent.'

'But you *did*. Because you made him bankrupt. Why? *Why?*'

Daniel Conrad sighed inwardly. He felt very sorry for this young girl, and she didn't really know what she was talking about. Fortunately, Crompton had explained over the 'phone what a state she was in. But Daniel couldn't really help her; there were certain matters he felt it best not to mention to her, certainly not now, while she was so terribly upset about her father's death. Perhaps he never would. It was best to let sleeping dogs lie.

'Not I, Miss Kent. Not personally. No one person made that decision. And nobody wanted it to happen. At the creditors' meeting, the consensus——'

'It was you. It was *you*.' Donna was hysterical. She had realised that it was in fact Daniel Conrad who had done this. It was him, personally. 'You *must* have been the instigator, you're the Financial Director here!'

'My dear girl, that doesn't make me autonomous! The board of directors——'

Again, she wouldn't let him finish. Beyond her hysteria one thing was very clear in her mind: there was nothing she could do. She was unable to change anything. Her father's good name had been tarnished, she was penniless but there was nothing she could actually do about it.

Frustrated beyond reason, all her anger and hurt was focused entirely on the man before her. 'You bastard! Well, I hope you're satisfied.'

If Daniel Conrad reacted to this, Donna never knew about it. She didn't hang around to find out. She fled from his office, out of the building, through the yard and into her aunt's car. She drove for about one mile then stopped because she couldn't see more than a few yards in front of her. Her tears came in a torrent. She sat in the car for a long time, sobbing hysterically until finally she was limp and exhausted.

During the days that followed she cried again, often. An inquest into Joseph's death was held in the Coroner's Court and resulted in an 'open verdict'. That was, Donna thought, better than a finding of accidental death but it still wasn't accurate, it should have been recorded as suicide.

She cried in the arms of her aunt and in the privacy

of her room at night. She cried until she could cry no more, until strength, both physical and psychological, began at last to return to her. Then, at least as far as the immediate future was concerned, she knew what she was going to do with herself.

'You must go home now, Auntie Liz.' She said this to her mother's sister one evening, when her mind had cleared enough so she could make decisions. 'I can cope now. I'm sure Uncle Desmond needs you and is missing you.'

Elizabeth didn't doubt that. 'But—but what are you going to do?'

'I'm going back to college, to finish my training.'

'Well, that's sensible, dear, but I meant what are you going to do about the house? When will you put it up for sale?'

Dumbfounded, Donna stared at her. 'For sale?' It had never occurred to her to do that. Not for an instant had she considered selling her home. 'Never! For heaven's sake, how can you think I'd do such a thing?'

Her aunt's mouth opened and closed helplessly. 'But—but it's the obvious thing to do, pet! This place is all the money you have in the world. Of course you must sell it. It's far too large for one person. What do you want four big bedrooms for? And all that garage space? And how would you cope with the gardens, all that ground? You couldn't afford to keep the gardener on, or the daily. Donna, you couldn't afford the upkeep of a place like this. Even the rates must be——'

'I know,' Donna snapped. Then, feeling very guilty, she hugged and kissed her aunt, apologising. 'I'm sorry, Auntie. You've been so good to me and I'm very grateful. I—it's just that I have to sort myself out now. I'm an adult and I shall learn to cope. I'm going to let the house.'

'You mean rent it? But what's the point?'

'It'll be a source of income,' Donna pointed out. She did not go on to say she would never, ever, part with this house. It wouldn't sound logical. It probably wasn't logical; it was emotional. But what of it? She had lived there since she was three years old and her father had been enormously proud of the place. Joseph Kent had pulled himself up by his bootlaces. In earlier years he had worked, physically, extremely hard in getting himself established. He had been something of a rough diamond but he had seen to it that his child had been brought up to be a lady, had been given a good education and any material thing she wanted. She had never gone short of love and affection, either.

No, she wasn't going to part with this house. In it there were only nice memories for her. Her parents had had a happy marriage and life here had been good for all of them. Besides, it was all that was left of the little empire that had once been her father's. And she was the only Kent left now. One day, one day she would come back to live in this house, when she herself had made her mark on the world.

She didn't voice any of these thoughts to her aunt. They might have sounded like so much pie in the sky. She had a long way to go to achieve her ambition, in the meantime she didn't even have so much as a car to sell. Her father's car had been written off in the accident. His company vehicles were to be sold, of course, to help raise the money for his debts, to pay off those who had destroyed him.

'Yes,' her aunt said thoughtfully. 'I suppose it will give you an income. But in the meantime you must let me help you financially. I can give you——'

'No. Thank you all the same,' she added gently. 'I have a few hundred pounds in my bank account. It'll be more than enough to see me through my last term at college. The fees and my board are already paid for. Then I'll get a job and I'll have the rent from the house. There'll be some money from Daddy's car insurance, too. Eventually. I don't know how much, his solicitor spoke to me about it and he's dealing with it.'

Elizabeth looked at her worriedly. The girl was

convinced her father had taken his own life but she herself was not of that opinion. 'Donna,' she said tentatively, 'I'm astonished that Joseph had never taken out any life insurance. I think——'

'He was only forty-three! Why should he have thought of it? After all, there's no mortgage on this house and he didn't have Mummy's welfare to think of.'

'No, but he had yours to think of, and I'm sure he must have. Don't you see, dear? He wasn't expecting to die. He didn't take his own life. I want you to get that out of your head. He wouldn't have done that to you, he loved you too much. Your Uncle Desmond spoke to him on the 'phone only a few days before the accident and he said how much he was looking forward to your coming home for Easter. It was an accident, Donna. A fluke. One of those strange things that happen sometimes. A slip of concentration, perhaps, and——'

'No,' Donna said firmly. 'My father didn't have lapses of concentration. He wasn't exactly senile!'

When Elizabeth started to say something else, Donna stopped her. She was not, she insisted, prepared to discuss that subject any further.

CHAPTER THREE

AUNT ELIZABETH went back to Rotherham the next day. Donna should have gone back to Eastbourne but she didn't. She had already missed the start of her last term but she wanted, needed, a couple of days of privacy, to be alone with her thoughts.

So she stayed in the house and roamed from room to room like a lost soul. The place was so empty now but so dear to her. The house comforted her somehow. She didn't want to leave it at all. Of course she had to; she had to finish her training and get the certificate which would help her to get a good job, a decent salary. Even so, and Aunt Elizabeth had been right in this, she would be hard pressed to pay the rates and maintain the house, let alone have help with the upkeep and the garden. No, she simply had to rent it, but not just yet. She would leave that till the summer. She would come back then and sort it all out, at the moment she couldn't bear the prospect of talking to an estate agent about it. She was too ... too tender at the moment, too delicate emotionally.

On the day she left for college, she covered everything with dust sheets, checked that everything was switched off and safe and locked up the house at eleven in the morning. The taxi she had ordered was waiting outside. The driver's face was familiar to her and he looked at her gravely.

'Good morning, Miss Kent. I want to say that I'm very sorry about your father. I read in the local paper about ... everything.'

'Thank you.'

'Back to the catering college in Eastbourne, is it?'

Donna frowned. From her seat in the back of the car she glanced at the man via his driving mirror. She knew

she had been in this taxi before, he might well have
been the driver who had taken her to the railway station
after the Christmas holidays. So it was fair enough that
he knew her name. But how did he know she was going
back to college and what sort of college it was? She
hadn't told him, she was sure of it. She didn't hesitate
in asking him.

'Your father told me, he said you were a smashing
cook already.'

'When?' she asked, puzzled. 'When did you see my
father?'

There was a shrug. 'He used our firm from time to
time. Taxis for customers, you know. But I gave him a
ride home one night when he was a little, er ...' His
voice changed slightly and he rushed through the rest of
the sentence as if that would make it less disturbing.
'. . . a little under the weather.'

'Under the weather? My father never had a day's
illness in his life!'

Donna's indignation brought the driver's eyes up to
his mirror. In her neat red suit with a matching hat she
looked a pretty little thing. God, but she was pale! Her
big blue eyes looked too large for her face. She'd
probably lost weight. And she looked worried to death
now; he wished he'd never opened his mouth. But he
had, so he realised he'd better explain and put her mind
at rest. 'I didn't mean that, miss,' he said uneasily. 'I
meant that—well, you know, one night when your
father had had a drop too much. We all do it from time
to time, don't we?'

The taxi driver had only made matters worse,
however. Over the next few minutes, Donna extracted
from him a story that astonished her. It seemed that her
father had been drinking in an inn called the Hare and
Hounds, a place Donna didn't know of, some twenty
miles away. The taxi driver had gone in for a drink, had
recognised Joseph Kent and had taken him home
because, the driver eventually admitted, he had been
'absolutely legless'.

She had known her father to take a drink but she had never known him to have too much. She had certainly never seen him drunk. 'When was all this?' she asked. 'It's important that you remember, please. Can you cast your mind back?'

'Cast my mind back?' The driver sounded surprised. 'It wasn't long ago. It was just a couple of weeks before his accident.'

'Oh.' The word came out dully. She had had the feeling that this had happened some time ago, that perhaps her father had had something else on his mind, apart from his bankruptcy. But it wasn't so, he had obviously drunk himself into oblivion because of his recent troubles.

Donna looked out of the window and they rode the rest of the way in silence. Nobody was more grateful for that than the taxi driver. It was clear to him by then that there were one or two things about Joseph Kent that his daughter didn't know. Well, he wasn't going to say anything else to the kid. It wasn't part of his business to spread rumours. And he had heard a few, he had heard a few!

Donna returned to the Wolds in the summer. She stayed at the house for only two nights. That was as long as she was able to stay because she had a job lined up. The college had got it for her, in fact. It was in the kitchens of a large department store, at their branch in Richmond. She had never been to Richmond, never been to London (except for a few hours in Heathrow Airport) until she went for her interview and sorted out some accommodation. She stayed in a hotel in Richmond for a couple of nights and she had gone into London to see a car someone had advertised, a cheap second-hand effort she felt she could afford. The insurance money for her father's car had come through all right but she wasn't going to spend all of it. Happily, the written-off car had been in Joseph's name and not his company's, otherwise the liquidator would probably have got his hands on the money and dished it out to her father's killers.

She was pleased about her job. As for living in Richmond, well, that didn't matter. If she couldn't live at home then Richmond was as good a place as any.

She didn't remove the dust sheets when she got back to Lincolnshire, except for those in her bedroom. There was no point. She would let the estate agent handle everything. She called in on her father's solicitor, who recommended some agents to her, then she spent time talking to the agents and listening to their advice. She also made it clear to them what she was and was not prepared to do with her property and its contents. In the months since her father's death she had become far more assertive than she'd ever been before. She wasn't going to stand for any nonsense from anyone over anything. Not ever. It was a hard world and she intended not only to survive in it but to succeed in it.

Her three days in Lincolnshire were very busy ones. She spent her time going from one office to another. She called on Joseph's accountant, Mr Crompton, by appointment this time . . . and he had news for her which drove her almost crazy with frustration.

'*What?*' She had been sitting with him for about ten minutes when suddenly she was on her feet again, glaring at him. 'Mr Crompton, I'm appalled!' How could you? To sell it to Daniel Conrad, of all people!'

The accountant groaned inwardly. He had the feeling of *déjà vu*. 'Donna, I've just told you, *I* didn't do it. It wasn't up to *me*. It's all under the control of the liquidator.'

Donna wasn't listening. She went up the wall, ranting. 'You sold Daddy's unfinished office block to Daniel Conrad! To *him*, of all the people in the world! And for such a pathetic price. Isn't it obvious to you what he'll do with it? He's got money, he'll finish the building and sell it at a big, fat profit. I shouldn't really be surprised by this but it never occurred to me that that bastard would put in a bid for it! Was he entitled to? I suppose he must have been. What a nerve, what a bloody nerve. And think of the money he'll make! Well that's just great! Handing over Daddy's property on a plate! By God, Daniel Conrad certainly had his eyes on the main chance, didn't he? The devious swine!'

Mr Crompton looked at her, wondering whether she expected an answer or whether this was another rhetorical question. She had changed since he'd seen her last. He wasn't surprised by her outburst but he was surprised by her language. He had always thought her a refined sort of girl, quite the young lady.

He did his best to calm her and he told her again that it was the liquidator's job, not his, to accept or reject any bids for her father's company assets. He also made it clear that the liquidator would get the best price he could and that if Daniel Conrad's bid for the office block was the best one, there was no reason it shouldn't be sold to him.

'Except on moral grounds,' she said. She did not sit down again. 'All right, Mr Crompton, all right. I'm going now. This isn't your responsibility, I know that really. It's just—I hope you haven't any more wonderful news for me? What about those unfinished bungalows in Market Rasen? Has Conrad bought those for a quarter of their worth?'

'No, no, no, Donna. Another builder bought them.'

'Probably a subsidiary of Conrads,' she said sarcastically.

Mr Crompton said no more. He felt exhausted after she'd gone. Her hatred of Daniel Conrad had made him flinch; it worried him to see such venom in the eyes of one so young. It didn't seem healthy. Had she heard any of the rumours? he wondered. They had started immediately after Joseph's death and they had been rife for some time. They had even reached his ears, and he was in Louth, which was some miles from the villages near the Kents' house.

No, he reasoned, she probably hadn't heard any gossip. She had been away at college for the past four months and it was all probably a nine-day wonder by now. People wouldn't still be nattering to one another about Joseph. And who knew whether there was any truth in their gossip-mongering, their speculations? He certainly didn't.

After leaving the accountant's office. Donna headed for the house in her second-hand car. She stopped in the nearby village and bought food for her dinner. Then she went to the post office and, finally, she called at the small sub-branch of the bank where her account was held. She wanted to give them instructions to transfer her account to Richmond.

Almost every face she encountered was known to her. She had called at these various places a hundred times in the past. Most of the people, assistants and other shoppers alike, smiled at her and asked how she was. Some merely nodded and glanced away, as if embarrassed. She found that hard to credit, but that's how it was. It was very obvious to her that a lot of gossiping must have gone on here.

But a couple of people actually snubbed her as she walked through the village's tiny shopping centre, that was something she absolutely did not understand. They were people she had known, albeit only at a distance, almost all her life. Being ignored by them, blatantly avoided, did not upset her, it infuriated her beyond description. What had she done to deserve it? Was there some sort of stigma attached to her now? Because her father was a bankrupt? Or because he had committed suicide? Or both?

Donna didn't waste any mental energy analysing their motives. She put it down to parochial narrow-mindedness and their lack of understanding of all the facts. One day, she would come back here permanently. She wasn't ashamed of anything at all, least of all her beloved father.

Early the next morning she packed into her car all her personal belongings. This still left a large crate full of things which stood in the hall and would be forwarded to her by rail in due course. The estate agents had said they'd be glad to oblige by doing that for her. Everything else was staying, every stick of furniture, just as it was. She wanted to let the house furnished, so that it would be lived in and looked after— by people who must supply excellent references.

When the doorbell rang she assumed it was the man from the estate agents', though she wasn't expecting him.

She certainly wasn't expecting Daniel Conrad, either, but there he was, on her doorstep, dressed immaculately and looking prosperous. Behind him was a shiny new car, parked on the drive . . . beside her old banger.

Donna was so stunned by his appearance that she simply couldn't speak. She knew she must have gone white, she could feel it happening to her. She felt faint.

'Miss Kent,' he said quietly, 'I'd like to talk to you. May I come in?'

She could do no more than stare at him. Somehow, in some corner of her mind, she registered that his eyes gave the illusion of gentleness. In one instant they looked brown, in the next instant they looked green. It was when he reached for her arm that she was jerked into a reaction. 'Don't!' she hissed. 'Do *not* touch me!' She stepped back swiftly, clinging to the door for support.

And then she tried to slam the door in his face but he put a foot in the way. Donna looked up at him with every ounce of her hatred showing in her eyes. She was five foot two in her bedroom slippers, a curvaceous but tiny eighteen-year-old who had matured physically as much as she was going to. He was six feet tall if he were an inch and judging by his build he probably weighed around thirteen stones. But she needed neither brawn nor brains to handle this man. All she needed was guts and she had plenty of those.

'Your foot, *Mister* Conrad. Remove it! I have nothing to say to you and you are *not* coming into my house.'

'Then just listen to me,' he said calmly. 'I want to talk to you about your father, about your accusations——'

'Go to hell. Don't you dare breathe the man's name. You're not fit to speak his name. Now get away from here!'

The foot was still in place. Daniel Conrad stood his ground in every sense. She wasn't going to slam the door in his face, he wasn't going to allow that. But whatever she did, he wouldn't lose his temper with her. She was obviously as stubborn as a mule and a little stupid with it, but he had to make allowances, given all the circumstances.

In any case, though he had been with her for only a minute he had realised that she hadn't heard any gossip at all. Her attitude would probably have been different if she had, almost certainly. The difficult thing was that he couldn't tell her anything, either. She wouldn't be able to handle it, that was obvious. She looked wild with fury as it was; he wasn't going to add to that fury.

'Miss Kent,' he said, 'believe it or not, I want to help you.'

An involuntary bark of laugher escaped from her, a hollow, bitter sound. 'Why of course I believe it, Mister Conrad. And how do you plan to do that? Supposing, that is, I needed help?'

'I believe you do,' he said, in that infuriatingly quiet tone. 'I got married last month. You probably didn't know that, and I——'

'Bully for you,' she cut in. 'Now take that foot away or else I'm going back into my living room and I'm going to call the police. You're trespassing on private property.'

Daniel removed his foot. He didn't doubt that she meant what she said and he could live without a scene with the police. That wouldn't get anyone anywhere. 'And I'm here to make you an offer for this house,' he persisted. 'My wife likes the look of it.' That wasn't true, but it didn't matter. 'She's seen it often from the road,' he went on, jerking his head in the direction of the lane at the end of the long, straight drive. 'I'll pay you, in cash, whatever you want for it, within reason. After all, it's been standing empty . . .'

As he spoke, Donna had what she could only describe to herself later as a temporary mental blackout. She was still on her feet, she was still looking at the man, but her ears simply switched off and for long seconds she could neither hear nor think.

It passed, it was replaced by a depth of anger which made anything she had experienced before weak by comparison. She couldn't speak. Not one syllable could she utter. While her mind screamed accusations at the man she held responsible for her father's death, she remained physically, totally, inert.

She wanted to ask him whether he were not satisfied with the damage he'd already done. You want this house, my home, as well as everything else you've taken? she asked silently. Do you want to drive everyone with the name of Kent out of this shire? Do you plan to end up owning the whole of Lincolnshire, or just those things that belonged to my father? What would you do with the house, Mister Conrad, redecorate and then sell it at a profit, just as you'll do with that unfinished office block you got for a song? Do you think you're God? You are sick, do you know that? You are a megalomaniac. You are *ill*.

But not a word passed her lips. She caught the end of his little speech: '. . . know you've planned on renting the place. I saw the ad in the paper this morning.'

Silently, Donna walked away from him. She went into the living room and picked up the telephone receiver. She hadn't even dialled 999 before she heard the door of a car slamming.

She put the receiver down again as Daniel Conrad's car took off down the drive. She watched it disappear from view, feeling, quite suddenly, an inexplicable urge to laugh. She wasn't even aware there were tears on her cheeks.

CHAPTER FOUR

Now, six years later, Donna was in a similar state. Similar but not the same. She wasn't standing by the window in her house, she hadn't even been back to visit the place in the last six years. She had visited her aunt and uncle in Rotherham and they had visited her in Richmond, but she had not been over the Lincolnshire border. The management of her house had been handled entirely by the agents and she communicated with them by letter.

No, she wasn't at home; she was sitting on the lavatory seat in the bathroom of a rather swish house which belonged to one of her customers, not that she realised quite where she was. She didn't hear the knocking on the bathroom door, she was so deeply engrossed in her memories, in her past. As in the past, she didn't even realise there were tears on her cheeks.

The knocking on the door got louder but it was only when someone started shouting her name that she snapped out of her trance-like state.

'Donna? Donna! For God's sake answer me! Are you all right?'

'Siggy?' She couldn't even be sure of that, she was so . . . so out of herself. 'Is that you, Siggy?'

'Who the hell do you think it is? Of course it's me, you idiot!' There followed a few choice words which should have made her blush, but didn't. 'I thought you'd fallen down the loo or drowned in the bath, or something. Get out here, will you? I've got a horde of hungry people on my hands and about three million steaks to cook. What do you think I am, a one-man bloody miracle worker?'

'All right, Siggy, all right. I'm coming.' She opened the bathroom door, unable to smile at his exaggerations,

48

his tantrum. Nor could she decide quite what she was going to do now. She wasn't sure she could bear to stay on the same premises as Daniel Conrad. On the other hand, Kieren was a good customer and she had a job to do.

'For heaven's sake, Donna, what are you playing——' Siggy stopped dead. 'Grief, you're as white as a sheet!' His attitude changed at once. 'Are you ill, love? What is it? What's wrong?'

'No, I'm not ill. I'm coming down now. Just let me wash my hands.'

'But you're—you're . . .' She was crying. Siggy was fazed. Tears? From Donna? This was something he had never seen, something he had never thought to see. It threw him, this was absolutely not his image of this girl and he didn't know how to handle it.

Donna made that unnecessary for him. 'Go down and start cooking, Siggy. I'm okay, I'll join you in a minute.' The look on his face made her feel sorry for him, made her feel she owed him at least some sort of explanation. 'Everything's cool now, honestly. I—it's just that there's someone here who . . . Let's just say it's someone whose path I'd never expected to cross again. Okay?'

Siggy nodded. He wouldn't probe any further. He retreated almost gratefully.

Donna washed her hands and face and pulled herself together. So Daniel Conrad was here, so what? She would cope. Kieren Gardner was spending a lot of money on this party and it was her responsibility to get on with her job. She was the one who shouldered responsibility with ease, wasn't she? She was the strong one, the boss. The evening would pass quickly enough and that would be the end of it. Daniel Conrad was probably down for the weekend, she told herself, just as Kieren's sister and brother-in-law were. She wondered vaguely about Conrad's wife; why she hadn't been on the arm of her husband when he'd walked into the drawing room earlier.

During the next couple of hours, in the gardens where Donna and Siggy were cooking, Daniel Conrad's presence made itself felt to her throughout every single minute. There were dozens of people milling about but it seemed that every time she looked up, it was him she saw. From a distance. Watching her. There was no sign of a wife; he didn't talk to any one person in particular, in fact he was standing alone for most of the time. He didn't seem very sociable, indeed he looked bored— except for his interest in her.

Around eleven o'clock, Donna slipped upstairs to the loo and when she emerged it was to find herself in a direct and private confrontation with him. He was sitting on a chair at the far end of the landing, near the stairs, one hand was in a pocket of his sports jacket and was fiddling with some coins.

The noise stopped as she approached, which she had no choice but to do. He stood, between her and the stairs. 'So we meet again, Miss Kent.'

'Excuse me. I have work to do.'

'The cooking's finished. Everyone's stuffed to the gills.'

Donna wouldn't look at him. 'Just the same, let me pass. I have nothing to say to you.'

'I want to talk to you.'

'Are you deaf, Mr Conrad?' She made herself look at him then, feeling, for the first time ever, just slightly intimidated by the size of him, the big bulk of him blocking her way. Her reaction infuriated her. 'Get *out* of my way!'

'There's no need for that tone of voice. You're no longer a young girl and in a state of paranoia.'

'Para . . .?' She couldn't finish the word. Her breath whooshed out of her furiously and she put one hand flat on his chest and shoved, hard.

He didn't even lose balance. He took hold of her wrist and thrust her arm away, his eyes suddenly flaring with the first hint of emotion she had ever seen in them. 'Cut that out!' he ordered. 'Be reasonable, for God's

sake. Six years have passed since your father died and
you're behaving as illogically now as you did then.
Put the past in the past, Donna, where it belongs.'

Coming from his lips, the use of her first name, the
very mention of her father was more than enough to
put her in a spin. She landed a very satisfying slap
across his face and it left him so momentarily stunned
that she was able to get away from him with ease.

She was shaking by the time she got downstairs.

'Donna?' It was Kieren. 'It's a great evening, isn't it?'
His arm came around her shoulders. She let it be.

She nodded, her voice barely more than a whisper.
'Yes, Kieren. It's a simply marvellous evening!'

Her sarcasm didn't go over his head. He looked at
her questioningly. 'What is it, Donna? It's got
something to do with meeting Dan, hasn't it? Where do
you know him from?'

'Lincolnshire. That's where I come from originally.'

'I didn't know that! I say, you weren't at Dan's
wedding by any chance?' Kieren seemed highly amused.
'I mean, have I met you in the past, when you were
sweet sixteen and never been kissed?'

'No, you didn't meet me at his wedding. And for the
record I was eighteen when he got——' She broke off.
She was saying too much. Nobody in the south knew of
her past. Not even Siggy, not much anyhow. Besides,
Kieren had had a drop too much and was chatting idly.
It was just another excuse to flirt with her. 'Excuse me,
Kieren, I must start clearing up a few things.'

'Will you have lunch with me on Monday?'

'No.'

'Will you come out with me for the afternoon,
tomorrow? It's Sunday, we can go for a trip on the
river.'

She couldn't help smiling at him. Persistence was
something she couldn't disapprove of in a person. 'I
have no time to go out with you or anyone else. So
you see, it's nothing personal. You're a lovely man
but I'm not interested, okay? Besides, you've got a

houseful of guests, you ought to be entertaining them tomorrow.'

'Guests? Oh, you mean my sister? She and her hubby are leaving for Scotland around noon. And Daniel, well, he doesn't count. He's big enough to look after himself, don't you think? Besides, he's been here for weeks. He's house-hunting, you know.'

House-hunting? For whom? Where? And why? She wanted to fire all these questions at her customer, but she wouldn't. She wouldn't be seen to be so interested in whatever Daniel Conrad was up to; Kieren might misunderstand. 'Excuse me,' she said again.

Most of the party guests had moved indoors by then; the late June evening had been beautiful, the weather just glorious, but it was chilly now. Donna and her staff cleared up, packed up and made their way back into the centre of Richmond.

Once they were in the yard at the back of the shop Donna jumped out of the van and got immediately into her car. She asked Margaret and Pauline if they wouldn't mind unloading the van without her, saying that Siggy would run them home. She was telling the truth when she added that she had a blinding headache.

She had only a short drive to her house, which was on the outskirts of Richmond. It was a tiny house with small rooms, three up and three down. Still, it suited her needs for the time being. It was in a quiet street, the middle of a row of terraced houses which were all nicely painted and looked after by their owners. Donna was buying hers on a mortgage from her bank. She had started her life in Richmond by living in various flats but that had been a rather noisy existence at times and not at all satisfactory. Besides, she didn't like forking out rent when she might as well be paying a mortgage. It was a far better investment.

What should have been her second bedroom was an office. What should have been her dining room was part stockroom, part guestroom. There was a bed-settee in it, a chest of drawers and two wardrobes which were mainly full of glasses and crockery—an overspill from the stockroom at work.

Apart from these two rooms with their unusual contents, the rest of the house was comfortable and nicely furnished. It was a small place but it was home, her sanctuary. She had taken care with her furnishings and decorations, they spoke of quality and her innate good taste. She was proud of her little house.

As soon as she got through her front door, she sank into an armchair. She was absolutely exhausted, not only by the long day but also by the scene with Daniel Conrad. By the very appearance of him, by all the memories he had resurrected. She felt drained, utterly drained.

She didn't move from her armchair for quite a while. She was trying to summon the energy to take her upstairs to bed, not that she would sleep. She was too disturbed for that, though she had a lot to do tomorrow and she must try to get some sleep.

For once she didn't take a bath before getting into bed, she usually needed one to ease her bones. She was aching tonight, true enough, but the ache was coming from somewhere far deeper inside. It wasn't due solely to her meeting with the Conrad man, not solely. Over the years she had managed to put things into perspective to a certain extent as far as he was concerned. The more she had learned about business, the more she had come to realise that if a firm allowed a customer, albeit an old-established one, to run up too big a bill, trouble could easily ensue. And if several customers happened to do it at the same time, which might well have been the case with Conrads, the firm's cash flow, or rather the lack of it, could quickly get them into hot water.

She had learned this from her own experience. She had had bad debtors in the past. To be fair, if in her imagination she magnified her own little business into one the size of Messrs Conrad, she could begin to understand that it was sometimes necessary to put pressure on one's non-paying customers. Nevertheless, she couldn't imagine herself ever forcing someone into bankruptcy. There again, she would probably never be in the position to be able to. She didn't deal in enormous amounts of money.

On balance, she was able to think of Conrads' action with more understanding and less anger than she used to. They had known it would mean the winding-up of her father's company but they could not have known it would lead to his literal, personal destruction, his death. Many bankrupts, and genuine ones at that, found a way of bouncing back to succeed another day.

What choked Donna, the ache that had never died inside her and was gnawing at her right now with renewed strength, was that her father had given up. *That* still hurt as much as ever. No, he had not left a note, but she was still convinced it had been suicide.

And so, on balance, while she could no longer reasonably accuse Daniel Conrad of her father's death, she could still hardly bear to look at the man. She couldn't accuse him, and yet ... and yet she would never be able to forgive him, either. Not that that conclusion made any sense. It was illogical, emotional, but she felt she was entitled. It was impossible for her to think of her father without thinking of Daniel Conrad, and vice versa. One man she loved, the other she hated.

With the aid of her repeating alarm-clock, Donna got up at eight on the Sunday. That was a lie-in for her. She wasn't exactly bright-eyed and bushy-tailed but she was functioning. She took a long, hot bath then got down to work, typing revised specimen menus. She and Siggy changed their menus every so often, especially when the seasons changed, and there were quite a number of them—menus for dinners, buffets, weddings and so on.

When the doorbell rang in what felt like the middle of the day, she glanced at her watch, frowning. She wasn't expecting anyone. She never was, not at home. It had to be Kieren. Did he think she would change her mind about lunch if he took the liberty of showing up on her doorstep? If so, he had another think coming.

She was halfway down the stairs when she had the idea of not answering the door. She shook herself mentally. What kind of cop-out was that? That wasn't her style. Since when had she been unable to handle the likes of Kieren Gardner?

But it wasn't Kieren Gardner. It wasn't even someone like him, it was a tall, broad man with dark blond hair and eyes which were—at least today—hazel in colour. He was wearing dark brown cords, a brown and white checked shirt which was open at the neck, and slung over his shoulder was a tan suede jacket, hooked on to his fingers. It was Daniel Conrad.

'Well?' he asked. 'Do I pass inspection?'

'You don't pass my threshold,' she countered. 'What the hell are you doing here?'

'As gracious as ever, I see.' He looked directly into her eyes. She could see herself in his eyes, in miniature, strangely angled. A trick of the light. The sun was streaming directly overhead. 'And you're beginning to bore me, Donna. I'm going to talk to you sooner or later. Let's make it now, shall we?' And with that he put one foot on her doormat, on her property, and all the balance and perspective she had managed to acquire over the years went right out of the window.

She countered his action as swiftly as she'd countered his opening gambit—with a good, hard, kick on the shin.

Even if she could have anticipated his reaction, it wouldn't have stopped her from doing what she'd done. She didn't anticipate it, though, and the next thing she knew, she was being lifted bodily by the shoulders of the old grey shirt she was wearing. By the time Daniel had stepped through the small porch and into her living room, her legs were kicking at thin air and she was screaming at him to put her down.

He did so. Literally, effortlessly, he flung her into an armchair. She was on her feet again in a flash. She was back in the chair even quicker. He stood before her and gave her a small push. It felt to her like a shoulder-wrenching punch and it knocked her off balance, back into the chair. 'Damn you! What the devil do you think you're doing?'

'I think we'll have a cup of coffee here before I take you out to lunch. I suppose there is a kitchen in this rabbit-hutch? No, don't move. You're going to stay in that chair till I say you can get off it. You may tuck your shirt back into your slacks, though, you look scruffy enough as it is. Are you always that pale or have you had an accident with a bag of flour?'

All she could do was gape at him. She didn't know where to start in answering him, his insults. Convinced she was about to suffer a heart attack, or at least burst into flames, she opened her mouth and breathed. She just breathed. It had got to the stage where she couldn't have moved if she'd wanted to.

In no time at all her trespasser was back with two mugs of coffee, a bowl of sugar and some milk on a tray. He put the tray on an end table and lowered his large body on to her two-seater settee, which suddenly made it look like merely an overgrown armchair. He was big, all right. At least, he was compared to her. He was also furious, she could see it in his eyes.

'I'm going to hand you some coffee in a moment,' he warned. 'See that it stays inside the mug, Donna, at least until you're ready to drink it.' Holding her stare, he paused for just an instant. His voice was calm enough but everything about his features, the tension in his body, told her he was more than angry. 'There will be no more slapping, no more kicking. Quite the little spitfire, aren't you? For someone who's no bigger than ten pence worth of copper. Well now let me warn you, Donna, if there's one more piece of mischief out of you I'm going to put you over my knee and I'm going to wallop you so hard that you won't be able to sit down for a month. If you think for one second that I'm joking, or exaggerating, try me.' And with that he got up and carried the mug of coffee to her.

It was steaming. It was tempting. But she hadn't thought he was joking. She left the mug where he put it, on the table by her chair. She felt defeated. 'All right, Mr Conrad, you win. State your business and then get out.'

'Not so fast. Your attitude is prohibiting my saying what I want to say. I have to—er—soften you up a little first.'

'I haven't the faintest idea what you're talking about.'

'Of course you haven't.' He smiled. To her astonishment he smiled and it chased from his eyes that horrible coldness which had been in them only seconds earlier. They were gentle again, not that they deceived her. 'Hence our lunch date,' he went on.

Donna's voice was so brittle it sounded awful even to her own ears. 'There's no way I'm having lunch with you. Say what you have to say, please. You might start by telling me how you got my address. From Kieren, I suppose?'

'The telephone directory. It doesn't take too much thinking about, does it? Why don't you calm down a little, try being reasonable for a change? Try acting like a human being, even if you can't act like a lady. Kieren didn't actually know your address. He tells me he's never been here.' His eyes flicked around the room, from the beige three piece suite to the hi-fi unit, from the self-coloured, dusky pink carpet to the plain, painted walls which were the colour of eggshells.

'If we ignore the size of this place, it's very nice,' he pronounced. 'I see you have style.' He looked back at her, his eyes moving slowly over her and telling her that her 'style' didn't extend to her appearance. 'Do you always wear that brown elastic band round your hair? Couldn't you change it for a blue one on Sundays?'

Donna's eyes closed and she said a silent prayer. Don't let me laugh, *please* don't let me laugh. Daniel

Conrad had put his question so seriously, with such an innocent look on his face that she simply couldn't help being amused. She managed to keep an impassive face, she didn't laugh. Nor did she speak. She couldn't trust herself to.

'There's one thing you have to understand,' he went on. 'I'm not like Kieren, good friends though we are. I don't take no for an answer. He tells me you refused his invitation for today and for tomorrow, but you will come out with me, Donna.'

He spoke so positively, so confidently she almost believed it. Almost. 'Miss Kent, to you, if you don't mind. I appreciate that it's a name you'd rather forget, but you never will. Kent. Never forget who I am, Mr Conrad. Donna *Kent*.'

'It seems to me,' he said quietly, 'that the sooner you change your name, the better.'

'What's that supposed to mean?'

'It means several things. They'll all wait till some other time.'

Some other time? What the devil was he talking about now? She asked him.

'You'll be seeing me from time to time over the next few months. I'm coming to live in the area. Well, approximately. Anywhere within a fifty mile radius of Uxbridge will do. I'm house-hunting at the moment.'

'Uxbridge?' The question was out before she could think. 'Why Uxbridge?'

'Because that's where the headquarters of Conrad Transport are situated. Conrad Transport and Haulage Limited.'

'Conrad Transport? I've never heard of it.'

'Yes you have, under it's old name—Greengate and Grey.'

She had heard of Greengate and Grey. Hardly a day passed when one didn't see either a van or lorry of theirs. 'Are you telling me that it's *your* company now? Have you bought them out? Is your father a director, too?'

'No. Dad's still in Lincoln, in the old business. This is

my baby, nothing to do with Dad.'

'I smell a family rift,' she said facetiously. 'What happened? Isn't your father ruthless enough for you?'

Daniel didn't rise to it. He smiled again, but without humour this time. 'We're still good friends. We're just different, that's all. Dad's very fixed in his ways, resistant to change, even changes for the better. Our ideas, our methods and ambitions——' Quite suddenly he broke off, his eyes fixed on an invisible spot on the wall, and in them was something which looked suspiciously like pain. 'I—what was I saying, Donna?'

She had to think about it. She had been distracted by the pain in his eyes, curious in spite of herself. 'That— that your ambitions are different, I think.' What was she *doing*, showing an interest in him? What was she doing by *feeling* curious?

She snapped out of it at once. She looked down at the mug in her hands, at her wristwatch. Was she off her head? She'd been drinking coffee and talking with Daniel Conrad, of all people, for almost an hour! He had to get out and get out now. Even if she hadn't so much work waiting upstairs, he wouldn't be welcome here!

'Look,' she said, 'you have to go now. I've got a lot of work to do.' She held up a hand. 'I'm telling you, asking you, civilly, okay? I want you to go, since you won't tell me what you really want to say to me.'

'No, I'm not leaving. That isn't the way I've planned my day.'

'But——'

'*No buts!*' he said, his voice suddenly sharp. 'Go and get changed, I'm not taking you out looking like that. And don't come back with that elastic round your hair. With those big blue eyes and that pale blonde mane, one has the impression that a halo would be more appropriate. Amazing how appearances can deceive, isn't it?' He grinned at her then, a villainous grin. 'I'll settle for your leaving it loose. Now off you go, it's almost one o'clock already.'

'Now look, Conrad——'

'Daniel.'

'Never!'

'No, just Daniel.'

She got to her feet, not knowing what she was going to do about him.

He got to his feet, too, and with one question he made it very clear that he would have his way. 'More mischief, Donna?'

She paled visibly at the threat in his voice. 'You would, too, I don't doubt it!'

'Then you're thinking straight and talking sense, at last.'

CHAPTER FIVE

'WHAT am I doing here?' Donna whispered the words, not realising she had spoken them at all. She was sitting outside at a riverside restaurant, watching the boats sailing down the Thames and refusing to look at the man who sat facing her.

'You're sitting in the sun, watching the river and taking a few hours off work. You've just ordered avocado vinaigrette to be followed by a shrimp salad. You seem to have forgotten there's a glass of wine in front of you and you've been refusing to look at me since we got here.'

She crossed her arms stubbornly and kept her eyes on the sailboats. She was wound up like a jack-in-the-box. She knew full well what she was doing in the literal sense, what she couldn't understand was *why*. Why, how, had she allowed herself to be manipulated like this? She had put up a fight before leaving her house, a purely verbal one in which she had shouted several unladylike words at Daniel Conrad and demanded that he leave her alone.

It had been like water off a duck's back. He had shaken his head wearily at her language, glanced at his watch then taken two steps towards her. At that point she had backed rapidly away, out of her living room and up the stairs which opened into the dining room. She had dragged off her clothes, pulled on a rust-coloured skirt and blouse, muttering to herself all the time she was doing so. She had not taken the band off her hair, nor had she asked where he was taking her for lunch. She wasn't even hungry. They had driven in silence in the big black Volvo and he appeared to be totally impervious to her hatred of him.

'All right,' she said now. 'I'm here, about to have lunch with you. So what is it you want of me?'

'All in good time, Donna, all in good time. Why don't you just relax and enjoy yourself?'

There was no answer to that. She picked up her wine and drank it straight off, without tasting it. 'I'll say this for you, you're as stubborn as they make them.'

'How odd,' he laughed. 'I was just thinking the same thing about you.'

Their starters arrived. They ate in silence. It wasn't until she started eating that Donna realised how hungry she was. When their salads arrived with a second bottle of wine she actually found herself relaxing a little. She couldn't understand it, it had to be the effect of the warm sun on her. It was, she admitted to herself, extremely pleasant to be eating good food, drinking fine wine and sitting outside in the sun. The river Thames was glinting in the light, the air was sweet and clear here and the general atmosphere was one of laziness, lack of haste. It certainly made a change for her.

'Enjoying yourself, Donna?'

'I'm not a masochist, Mr Conrad. No, I am not enjoying myself. The food's good but the company's rotten.'

'You're beginning to make me angry again,' he said quietly, 'I've asked you to call me Daniel, haven't I?'

She looked at him then, scowling. 'This company you've bought, Greengate and Grey, were they in trouble? On the verge of going bust or something?'

'Now why should you think that?'

'Need you ask?' she said scornfully. 'I happen to know you have an eye for a bargain—like that unfinished office block of my father's in Louth, for example.'

'I could give you other examples, too,' he countered. 'I make no apology for buying that, so don't expect one. It had to be sold, I put in the highest bid, I got it. I contracted a builder to finish it and——'

'And sold it for a big, fat profit.'

'Not so fat. Just a reasonable return on my money. It was business, Donna, good business pure and simple.

There was nothing personal in it.' He was very serious now, watching her with interest. 'You asked about Greengate and Grey. No, they weren't about to go bust but they had suffered from mismanagement. They were an old-established company, run by two chaps who were getting past it and a general manager who, it turns out, was on the fiddle.

'Every aspect of the firm was out of date; they spread themselves too thinly, covering too large an area for their limited fleet of vehicles. Suffice it to say they didn't resist my takeover bid. I paid them a fair price and I bought their goodwill and their name—which I shan't be using. Shortly, all the vehicles will be overhauled or replaced, certainly added to, and the name Greengate and Grey will be replaced with the new company name. In the meantime I've got a lot of hiring and firing to do, offices to sort out and an extension to plan. To mention but a few things. Now what else would you like to know?'

'How long is it since you left your father's company?'

'Four years. I'm still on the board in an advisory capacity.' He shrugged. 'When it comes to time and motion, finances and investments, I happen to be something of an expert.' He left her no room for sarcasm; he had spoken neither modestly nor immodestly. 'I've discovered over the years that my expertise is in taking an existing business and improving it. I've bought and sold several companies since you and I first met.'

'I see. Quite the successful business man, aren't you?'

'I'm a very successful business man.'

She looked at him quickly. Their eyes held for several seconds, hers growing darker as her resentment of him made itself plain.

'Why don't you say it, Donna? Come on, stop playing games. We've made some progress today, you've even mentioned your father to me. Why don't you say the rest of it? Why don't you tell me how much you resent my success?'

His choice of words startled her. She pushed her plate away, her food unfinished. 'I—it isn't your success I resent, it's——'

'Me? Me, personally?'

'Yes. It's you personally.'

'But why? Why? It doesn't make sense.'

'I—I suppose not. I—it's just . . .' It was just that—what, exactly? She could no longer accuse him of being responsible for her father's death; she'd exorcised that idea some time ago. Keeping her emotions out of it, common sense had helped her to do that. 'I'd like to go home now. Please.'

'No,' he said simply, not taking his eyes from her. 'I'm looking forward to strawberries and cream and several cups of coffee. You'll stay put and you won't leave my sight until you tell me what's really going on in your mind.'

'But why should that matter to you?' she asked impatiently.

'It'll help you. Let's talk about the past and then we can forget it. Maybe there are a few things you didn't understand at the time. Ask me. Talk to me. *Communicate* with me, Donna.'

For several long seconds she looked at him curiously. His eyes were appealing to her. He seemed, he actually seemed concerned. She couldn't understand this invitation, she couldn't understand why he should care about helping her. Nevertheless, she started talking and once started it was as though she couldn't stop. In six years she hadn't talked to anyone about her father's bankruptcy—and now she was having lunch with the man who had brought it about.

They talked for an hour in great detail. Donna was shocked to learn that her father had owed Conrads more than a quarter of a million pounds. It made the action they'd taken inarguable. His credit limit had been half that and they had given him time, and more time, in which to pay. This, without cutting off his supplies until they had to.

'We had several other problems at that particular time,' Daniel informed her. Watching closely for a reaction, he asked, 'Do you know anything about them?'

'No,' she said truthfully, a little nonplussed. 'How could I? What problems?'

He was silent for a moment. Then he looked away and shrugged it off. 'Oh, other debtors, that sort of thing. Our own business was in a tricky position. And my father was unwell at the time.' His eyes moved back quickly to hers. 'Did you know anything about that?'

She had no idea what point he was trying to make, if any. What had this to do with anything? 'I know he ended up in hospital with ulcer trouble or something.'

'Where did you hear that? Who told you?'

She frowned at the intensity in his tone. She didn't need to think about her answer. 'From one of your employees. The day I came to your office. One of the men in the warehouse.'

Daniel said nothing to that. He waited, as if she might add something else. But there was nothing else Donna could add, nothing else she knew about it. Feeling suddenly self-conscious under his scrutiny, she heard herself saying, 'Perhaps I'll have some strawberries, too.'

He nodded and signalled the waitress, turning back to her at once. 'Is there anything else you want to ask me, Donna, anything else you want to say about all that business?'

She sighed. God, she was tired suddenly. And she'd had too much wine. She was tired, bone-weary . . . but she was relaxed. He had been right; talking about the past, most especially to him, had helped her to feel better about the whole thing. It had hung over her head for six years and she had finally got some answers, very sensible answers, straight from the horse's mouth, as it were. 'No, there's nothing else I want to ask you. It's just——'

'Go on.'

'It doesn't matter.'

But Daniel Conrad wasn't having that. 'Go *on*, Donna. Say it.'

She tried to, and he waited patiently, watching her struggle with it. She could feel tears prickling at the back of her eyes and the last thing in the world she wanted was to cry in front of this man. But he was a tenacious, persistent devil. She had to answer him anyway, so it might as well be with the truth. 'It's just that it still hurts,' she whispered, choked. 'It hurts like hell that I wasn't enough for Daddy to live for, that he took his own life.'

Daniel's swift intake of breath brought her eyes up to his. He looked stunned. He had paled visibly. 'God in heaven, do you still think *that*? Do you mean to tell me that six years later, you still think Joseph committed suicide?'

'I don't know why you look so appalled, Mr Conrad. What else am I supposed to think? Even the Coroner couldn't come up with a verdict of accidental death.'

Before anything else could be said, the waitress came up to them. Daniel gave their order and as soon as she retreated, he reached for Donna's hand.

She pulled it away, staring at him in bewilderment. 'I'm perfectly all right. There's no need for that, thank-you!'

He sighed. 'Sorry, I meant no offence. You—I ... God, it never occurred to me that you'd go on thinking it was suicide! I thought that was just your hysteria of the moment. All this time, all this time!' He seemed genuinely upset. 'Don't you see? The Coroner had to give an open verdict because there was no evidence one way or another. But it was an accident. It *was* an *accident*, believe me.'

'That's enough, please!' She held up both hands as if in defence. She was feeling slightly queasy, wishing she hadn't ordered the strawberries. 'Don't let's talk about it any more. *Please!*'

When he murmured his agreement, she began

instantly to feel better again. Soon it would be over, forever. Once and for all. He had finally said what he'd wanted to say to her since meeting her at the barbecue last night. Soon she would be home and safe and able to concentrate on the present.

She glanced at Daniel as he tucked into his strawberries. So he wasn't as shallow and as ruthless as she had thought him, after all. Her violent reaction on seeing him last night had bothered him. He had wanted to clear the air. Well, that was decent of him, she supposed. She couldn't approve of his kidnapping her in order to talk to her, but still. It wasn't important now.

'Donna?'

She opened her eyes. Her strawberries were in front of her, untouched. She blinked. Heavens, she had almost fallen asleep as she sat! She picked up her spoon and ate.

After two cups of coffee each, they left. They didn't talk in the car. There was no more to say. But there wasn't an atmosphere between them, not now. There was, simply, nothingness. She no longer hated Daniel Conrad but she could never bring herself to like him, either. No way. She simply disliked the man, with his strong-arm tactics and his stubbornness.

When he pulled up at her front door, parking immediately behind her car, she thanked him for the meal. 'I won't say it was pleasant, Mr Conrad, but I appreciate what you were doing. So good luck, goodbye and thanks.'

With a gentleness that surprised her, he said, 'Not so fast, please.' When she turned to look at him, confused, he went on, 'That talk we've just had. To be honest, I hadn't realised how necessary it was. Not fully. I still want to talk to you about another matter, but it can wait. Maybe till tomorrow, maybe next weekend or the weekend after that. We'll just have to see what progress we make. So far so good, I'd say. How about you?'

She was instantly suspicious, instantly on guard again. 'Now what are you talking about?'

'Our lunch date tomorrow. I'll collect you from your shop at noon.'

'I have a customer coming at noon. Not that it's relevant.' she added. 'I've just said goodbye to you, Mr Conrad, but in case you didn't hear me, I'll say it again. *Goodbye.*' She got out of the car and walked hurriedly to her door, fishing in her bag for her key.

Unperturbed, Daniel wound his window down. 'Then we'd better make it one o'clock,' he called to her. 'Don't worry, I won't keep you out long, I have a lot to do myself during the afternoon.'

'I'm not worried,' she hissed when she could find her voice. What an audacity he had! Was he deaf or was he daft? 'Because you won't be keeping me at all!'

She had to shout the last sentence because he'd already started driving away. But she knew he'd have caught it.

She went straight upstairs, stripped off her clothes and got into bed. She was in no fit state to work, thanks to him. Her mind was tumbling with all sorts of thoughts. All right, maybe Daniel Conrad wasn't as ruthless as she'd thought but he was certainly peculiar. What did he *want* of her, for God's sake? There was no point at all in sitting down to work now. The afternoon was shot, she'd had too much wine. She must have. How else could she have talked to Daniel Conrad for several solid hours?

She was exhausted. Compared to her normal working day, this one had been short. Yet she felt drained, weak. She hadn't finished the specimen menus, she hadn't even typed out the worksheets for tomorrow. Well, she'd just have to get up earlier in the morning and do them. She would finish the menus after her nap.

There was no way she was having lunch with him again, tomorrow or any other day. After a six year gap, she had crossed paths with him by sheer coincidence and she had, she admitted, benefited from the encounter.

But that was the end of it.

She never had lunch with anyone other than customers. She certainly didn't have lunches with men she didn't like. She most definitely didn't have lunches with married men she didn't like. Or any other kind of married man.

CHAPTER SIX

DONNA was writing notes. Her customer had been gone for just ten minutes when Siggy walked into her office. It was one o'clock exactly, not that she was aware of it.

'Hi, Siggy.' She looked up at him, hovering in the doorway of the tiny room. 'What's up? Aren't you feeling better after your meditations?'

'I was, but I've been serving in the shop for the past hour. Remember me?'

She smiled. Pat, one of their assistants, was off with a summer cold so Siggy was behind the shop counter, helping to deal with the usual lunch-time crowd who came in for pies and things.

'Anyhow,' Siggy went on, 'I trust your lunch date isn't going to take too long. You've got Mrs Jackson coming in at two-thirty about her daughter's engagement party.'

'I know it, darling, don't worry. I'm—*what* lunch date?' She was on her feet at once. Surely he hadn't turned up? Surely he hadn't had the gall actually to come for her after what she'd said?

He had. And Siggy looked very disapproving. 'What lunch date? It's that big lug who was watching you at Gardner's barbecue the other night. Six feet tall by six feet wide, I'd say. Mr Universe. Got it? He's standing in the shop right now and he's asking for you.'

'I don't believe it!'

'Believe it, love. What shall I tell him? Shall I . . .'

Donna listened to the suggestion Siggy made. She grinned. 'No, don't put it in quite those words! Tell him there's been a misunderstanding. I wasn't expecting him and I'm still with my customer.'

Siggy nodded and retreated. He was back in no time at all. With his arms waving about as he relayed Daniel

70

Conrad's answering message, the poor dear wasn't at all pleased. 'You'd better do something, Donna! I've got a shop full out there and I can't budge him.'

'Well, what did he say, for heaven's sake?'

'He said there's no misunderstanding, that he told you *very clearly* he'd collect you at one. He said your customer was due here at noon and he doesn't believe for one moment that you're still talking to him or her.'

They looked at one another helplessly. Siggy leaned against the doorjamb, a look of curiosity on his face. He was wondering who this big fellow was and why he seemed able to break through Donna's cool veneer. First he had made her cry, now he was making her furious.

'Oh, really? Right! I'll deal with this. Siggy, you carry on.' She pulled on the jacket of the suit she was wearing, smoothed back her already imprisoned hair, squared her shoulders and brought herself up to her full five feet two. Five feet four, thanks to the heels on her shoes. Enough was enough! Mr Daniel Conrad was going to have one or two things made very clear to *him*!

The pâtisserie was packed. Daniel was standing at the far end of the shop, near the inner door which led to the kitchen and office.

Donna flung the door open and found herself immediately face to face with him. 'Mr Conrad, you amaze me,' she said without preamble. 'I refused your invitation yesterday and I'm refusing it today, thank you all the same. I have a great deal to do and——'

'And you should have planned your day accordingly,' he interrupted. He was wearing an off-white jacket and dark brown slacks and his presence was catching the attention of two or three office girls who came in regularly for their lunch. 'I did. I've looked at three houses in three different areas this morning—but I got here bang on time. Good planning, I call it. Now then, I'll give you a few minutes to say farewell to your customer—if indeed there still is a customer—and then I'm coming into your office to get you.'

'There isn't a customer,' she admitted impatiently.
'but I simply haven't got time to lunch with you.' Her
eyes flicked past him, around the shop. Siggy was
managing both to serve someone and watch her at the
same time, and two old ladies with shopping baskets
were listening to her conversation, making no attempt
to hide the fact.

'Then make time,' he said, unmoved.

'Mr Conrad——' She broke off, flushing as two of
the office girls giggled. 'This is hardly the place to hold
an argument!' she hissed at him.

'Who's arguing? Go and get your handbag, you're
coming with me now, and that's that.'

'Now look——'

She had been going to say something about making
life easier for them both if he would just learn to take
no for an answer. But she never got that far. Nor did
she anticipate what he would do, there was no way
anyone could have been prepared for that.

Daniel Conrad merely sighed, as if bored. He took
his hands from his pockets, muttered something
unintelligible, bent down and took hold of her by the
waist. One second later she found herself flung over his
shoulder like a sack of coal.

Donna shrieked loudly, hardly able to assimilate
what had happened, why suddenly she was upside
down and a long way from the ground. She heard the
giggles of the office girls, the gasps of the old ladies
and a male customer saying, 'That's the way to
handle 'em!'

There was also Siggy's indignant, 'Hey, now wait a
minute!' Then there was the noise of the traffic as
Daniel stepped into the street with her and turned left.

'For pity's sake, put me down, Daniel! Put me down!'
She couldn't move her legs; he had one arm around
them and his other hand was planted firmly on her
bottom, holding her in place. Never in her life had she
felt so humiliated. This, in one of the main shopping
streets of Richmond, where so many people knew her!

What would they *think*? With her fists she beat against his back, yelling at him, cursing him.

He took not the slightest notice of her.

He walked on, she had no idea where he was heading. For all she knew, his car might be parked miles away. So Donna gave up and kept still. What else could she do? She was attracting enough attention as it was, without screaming to attract more. Even the policeman who walked past them didn't bat an eye! He must have assumed it was a lovers' spat or that she'd hurt her ankle or something.

'Right.' When they'd walked some three hundred yards, Daniel stopped outside an Italian restaurant. Donna was known in there, too, she'd eaten there often over the years. 'Have I to carry you in here or are you going to come quietly?' he asked, sounding like a police-officer making an arrest.

'I'll walk in, thanks.' Her voice was tight, barely audible. He'd won. Again. There was no way she could escape him, even when he put her down. She had accepted that fact a hundred yards ago, when she'd stopped yelling. 'I'll get you for this, Conrad, if it's the last thing I do!'

'What was that? Your voice sounds funny. Did you say you'd prefer me to carry you in?'

'I said . . . damn you! I'll *walk* in!'

When he plonked her on her feet, red-faced and breathless, she was so disorientated that she swayed against him. He made no move to help her, to get hold of her, he just allowed her to fall against the solid wall of his chest, grinning as he watched.

'You—bastard!'

'Tut-tut, Donna. I'm no such thing. If you'd swayed in the other direction, I'd have caught you. I'm nothing if not chivalrous.'

She was speechless. She looked at him with loathing but even that was pointless because by then he'd turned his back and was opening the door of the restaurant. She didn't bolt, as he knew she wouldn't, she just walked past him as he held the door for her.

'A table for two, is it, sir?'

Daniel shot her a pointed look as he addressed the head waiter. 'We're a few minutes late but I have booked. The name's Conrad.'

They were no sooner seated than the drinks waiter appeared. 'I'll have a gin and tonic,' Donna informed him, not even looking at her host. 'A large one.' She wasn't sure how she would handle that, not being in the habit of drinking the hard stuff during the day, all she knew was that she needed a stiff drink.

'Cancel that.' Daniel's voice cut across hers almost before she'd finished giving her order. 'Bring us a bottle of champagne, the best you have.'

She kept quiet even after the waiter had left them. She was bearing in mind that she was in a public place; she'd had quite enough humiliation for one day. She didn't want anyone else staring at her. But that wasn't likely, actually, not here. They had been seated in a booth at the back of the restaurant, where they were private. It was something else Daniel Conrad had probably planned.

He sat back in his seat and smiled at her.

'You needn't look so satisfied with yourself,' she snapped, keeping her voice low. 'Unless you actually derive pleasure from making people miserable.'

'I've no intention of making you miserable, little lady. Speaking of little ladies, who's the chap in your shop?'

She looked at him in disgust. 'That's Siggy.'

'*Siggy?* What sort of name is that?' He seemed highly amused now. 'Are we talking about the same person? I meant the little fellow with the permed hair and the cuban heels. Your cook.'

'That's Siggy,' she repeated. 'Siegfried Gee. And he would not take kindly to being referred to as a cook. For your information he's a master chef, pastry-making is his speciality. That, and his loyalty to me.'

'I see.'

'I don't think you do, Mr. Conrad.'

'Ah, but I do. It's Daniel, by the way. You've managed it once, keep trying. Now your Siggy, as you call him, is——'

'*Please*, leave it! I won't hear a word against him, I don't wish to hear any criticism of him. He's a lovely person, he's hard-working, conscientious and loyal. He also happens to be a friend of mine.'

It was as if he couldn't help himself, couldn't resist provoking her further. 'Well, that's all he'll ever be to you, that's for sure!'

'God in heaven, you are hateful, *hateful*! Just bear in mind that it takes all kinds to make a world, even your kind.'

'And what kind am I?'

He'd asked for it. She gave it to him. 'You're uncouth, ill-mannered and ill-bred. You are *the* archetypal, typical, male chauvinist *pig*! You're exactly the kind of man I dislike on principle. You and your sort leave me cold, stone cold.'

'I'm sorry I asked.' He seemed to be suppressing laughter now.

It infuriated her even further. 'You will be, because I haven't finished yet. You're arrogant, you're conceited and—I've just learnt—a bigot, a narrow-minded bigot!'

He gave her that look of pure innocence he'd given her the previous day. 'What? Just because I'm not smitten with your Siegfried?' And with that he roared with laughter. He laughed loud and long and she hated him more and more with every passing second. She also felt renewed gratitude that nobody could actually see them sitting together.

Only when the waiter came with the menus did he sober. Donna took hers and made a pretence of looking at it. She was so angry she could hardly see, all the printed words were running into one. 'You might as well order for me, she said at length. 'Since you're so good at taking charge of people.'

'Donna! I don't know what you mean. You and I had a date today. It was fixed. I couldn't let you back out at the last minute, it was unfair of you to try. Now *that* was ill mannered of *you*. I mean to say, a chap goes to all that trouble to spend his lunch-time with a pretty girl, then she tries to stand him up!'

She could do no more than stare at him. How did she begin to answer all that? She sat in silence. He ordered, and a moment later the champagne arrived. 'Would you mind telling me what this is in aid of?'

'This is a celebration, of course.'

'Of what, may I ask?'

'You may. It's a celebration of my finding a nice house to live in. It was the third house I saw this morning, and it's just the job, just what I want.'

'Just what *you* want? And what about your wife? Where is she, by the way? The poor dear. I didn't see her at the barbecue, or had you had a row that evening? I shouldn't be surprised, if you treat her the way——'

She broke off very abruptly. She had been fiddling with the stem of her champagne glass and it was only when she glanced at him that she knew she'd said something terribly wrong. There was pain in his eyes again, unmistakable this time. He was looking at her in disbelief, as though she had been talking to him one minute and the next minute she had stabbed him under the table. Unconsciously, her hand went to her mouth. 'I—I think I've to take it that you're no longer married . . .'

His nod in the affirmative was the barest movement of his head. 'I—suppose there's no reason you could know, should know. I thought maybe Kieren had mentioned . . . My wife died, Donna. She died of leukaemia just two years after we married, almost to the day.'

The ensuing silence was excruciating. Donna was far more affected by the news than she would ever have dreamt possible. She ought not to care, she ought not to be feeling anything. But the pain in Daniel Conrad's eyes touched her deeply. That and the realisation that his wife could have been only—what? In her mid-thirties at the most? Daniel was probably in his middle thirties now, in fact, so it was fair to assume that his wife would have been . . . 'I'm sorry,' she said, suddenly realising the words were long overdue. They were very sincere, too, and he knew it.

'Thank you.'

'I—did you have—I mean, have you got any children?'

He spoke so quietly she could barely catch the words. 'No, we planned . . . I mean, we planned not to have any. That is . . . could we leave this one alone, Donna? Some other time, perhaps.'

She nodded, only too relieved to change the subject. Things had levelled off between them somehow. Her anger had been swept aside by the turn in their conversation. With a determined effort, she picked up her champagne glass. She had made up her mind not to drink any but she had changed her mind. 'To your new home then, Daniel. I wish you well in it.'

There was the slightest pause as Donna waited, her glass poised in mid air. Then, his eyes not leaving hers for a second, Daniel raised his glass and they drank. She felt momentarily confused as she sipped at the cold wine, wishing she could know what he was thinking right then. 'Are you—well, you're obviously planning to stay in the south, since you've bought a house here.'

'Why not, I ask myself? I have a lot of contacts down here in the south, and I have some good friends, like Kieren. I suppose I could run the company at a distance, but why bother? I have no ties. I like Surrey very much.' He shrugged. 'By the way, the house is in Chertsey and it isn't exactly bought, not yet! I made the vendors an offer this morning. They might refuse.'

'And if they do? Will you increase your offer?'

'Maybe. I like the house but I don't feel that strongly about it.'

It was inevitable. Donna had been plunged into the past again, it was as if Daniel sensed it. 'What are you frowning about now, Donna? Are you eighteen years old again, by any chance?'

'I'd like to know,' she said slowly, calmly, 'why you wanted to buy my house in the Wolds. Was your—were you really in love with the look of it?'

'I liked it, yes. I told you at the time, I'm telling you again: I wanted to help you. I knew your financial situation—who didn't? To be absolutely honest, I felt sorry for you. I thought that a quick sale, a cash sale at a good price, might help you out. It would have.'

'Except that there's no way I'd part with the place.'

'You still own it? It's still let?'

She nodded. 'Off and on. It was supposed to give me an income but that proved to be a theory.'

Daniel was ahead of her. 'Bad tenants? Non-payment of rent?'

'One case of that, in spite of excellent references. People are funny, aren't they? Would you believe that I let the place to a writer and his wife and they neglected it abominably? I had to have it redecorated throughout. He was quite well known, too, said he was living in the Wolds for the purposes of research.'

'Yes, I'd believe it. As you rightly pointed out earlier, it takes all kinds.'

'The main problem has been that I couldn't let it continuously. Not everyone wants to live in the Wolds. It's not exactly in a prime position for a professional person, say. Someone who can afford the rent. It's quite a way from Lincoln, even Louth, all the busy areas where employment is. I didn't think of that at the time. Still, I haven't lost money. I haven't made a profit, but I haven't lost any.'

'You should sell the place. It belongs in your past, Donna.'

She looked at him, her eyes narrowing, not because of his remark but because of something he'd said the previous day. 'Just a minute, Daniel. How come you were able to offer me cash for my house when Conrads were in a "tricky" position financially?'

Her question surprised him. 'It was nothing to do with the company. I had private money, money my maternal grandmother left me. I'm referring to my natural mother's mother, by the way.'

'What?'

'I mean, I wasn't referring to Delia's mother.'

'Delia?' The name evoked the memory of Richard Conrad's wife. Donna had met her once, just once, as far as she could remember. She had been very young at the time, thirteen or fourteen, perhaps. Delia and Richard Conrad had come to the house for drinks along with some other couples. Maybe it had been someone's birthday, she couldn't be sure. Delia Conrad was memorable, though, in that she had very beautiful hair, a striking shade which is usually referred to as red. Indeed it was, almost literally, red, but apart from that Donna could remember little. 'So Delia isn't your natural mother. It never occurred to me. I had no idea.'

'She married Dad when I was nine. My sister was five at the time, our mother died giving birth to her—there were complications. Delia and my father didn't have any children of their own. Did you ever meet her?'

'Once, as far as I can remember.'

'She's very dear to me, a wonderful person. When my wife's illness was diagnosed, it was the things Delia said to me that gave me strength, the extra, special sort of strength which I needed to give Amanda support, to face the situation bravely . . .'

They lapsed into silence, each going off into their own thoughts. Donna sipped at her champagne. It was delicious, but what was she doing, drinking it in the middle of the day? What was she doing being here? What had she been doing sharing his pain? And she had shared it, fleetingly. As if spellbound she had watched all the amusement drain from his face when he'd talked about his wife, had watched his eyes darken so they had changed from hazel to brown.

And, now, they were gentle on her.

The following hour was neither comfortable nor

uncomfortable for her. The restaurant food wasn't up to its usual standard, as it happened, but then what was normal about today? As a result of this, she and her host got on to the subject of food and stayed with it. It was a safe, neutral subject. It was also something Donna knew a lot about and before she knew it, she was talking about the catering college she'd gone to, telling him with much amusement that the first thing they had taught her was how to make lentil soup.

'Lentil soup! It became a joke with us, you can imagine. All the students, that is. I mean, how basic can you get?' She chuckled at the memory. 'Still, that was the beauty of the place, they were very thorough. Nevertheless, and our teachers used to say this, until you're out in the world and earning your living in the kitchen, you don't really know what it's all about. Catering for a family is one thing, catering for fifty is quite another. Do you know, we students couldn't get away with anything! Apart from the practice, there was the theory. Heavens, I ended up with a pile of exercise books this big. Don't grin, I'm not exaggerating. I've still got them. Everything had to be planned beforehand, everything had to be written down. And I mean everything, from the time you'd planned on lighting the oven to the time you'd planned on serving the dish. Everything we wrote down got marked in red ink and I remember once losing marks in a test because I was being "uneconomical" in . . . in . . .'

Her hand was covering her mouth again. 'Sorry.'

'Don't be.'

She was actually blushing. What on earth had come over her? How could she have rambled on like that? He must think her mad! 'I'm—it must be the champagne.'

'I don't doubt it,' he said kindly, reaching to move her hand from her lips. 'I enjoyed your stories, Donna. More than you'd believe,' he added quietly. 'It's good to see you relaxed. Kieren's told me you're a maniac for work.' He was about to tease her, to tell her that for once her face wasn't so pale. Her cheeks were pink now.

But he thought better of it, she'd had enough provocation for one day. He didn't tell her either that she looked very lovely just now, in spite of that awful hairstyle.

The girl intrigued him. More and more, she intrigued him.

She looked vulnerable at that instant, incredibly so. Touchingly so. He took a surreptitious glance at his watch. Damn! He had to leave in fifteen minutes. 'Donna, I'm sorry to say I'll have to go shortly, I've got——'

'Aha! So that's the way to get rid of you, by boring you! Well, that should be easy enough.' She was half serious, half joking, she was certainly not herself right now. The champagne was affecting her.

Daniel grinned at her. 'You couldn't bore me if you tried, now shut up and listen. I'm taking you out for the day on Sunday, not just to lunch but for the whole day, got it? I dread to think how long it is since you had a whole day off.'

'Forget it.' His words had sobered her considerably. 'Absolutely *not*. It's out of the question. And don't try turning up at my house because I simply won't answer the door to you. You can't——'

'Then I'll huff and I'll puff and——'

'You can't,' she persisted, ignoring the amusement in his eyes, 'talk me into this one, Daniel. I don't want to see you ever again. I've stopped blaming you for Daddy's death, we've cleared the air very successfully— I'm even calling you Daniel, though it doesn't exactly come trippingly off the tongue! Please stop laughing, I mean what I'm saying. If I have to spell it out for you this time, so be it: I will not see you again. I do not like you.'

'But that's not true!'

She was starting to get irritated all over again. Bother the man! 'It is true. I thought I'd made it perfectly clear earlier.'

'But you know me better now than you did then.'

Impossible, the wretched man was *impossible*!

'The trouble is,' he informed her, his eyes growing serious, 'you still resent me. It isn't dislike, it's out and out resentment.'

'*No*,' she insisted, trying to hold on to reason. 'I've stopped resenting you, truly I have.'

'Then what is there to dislike about me?'

Donna flopped back in her chair. Had she thought Kieren Gardner was persistent? What a joke! He was a lamb compared to this man. She'd been amused by Kieren's persistence but it was not funny coming from Daniel Conrad. 'Your tactics, man, your *tactics*. I dislike the way you go about things. What about today's performance, for heaven's sake!'

Daniel put his elbows on the table and his face in his hands. 'You wound me, Donna. Oh, the irony! Oh, the injustice! I only use such tactics, as you call them, when you make it necessary for me to do so.'

Why didn't she get up and walk away? she asked herself. Why was it that this innocent act of his, his sheer temerity, almost fascinated her? She had never met anyone like him in her life! 'You can't be real. I must be having a nightmare.'

He laughed softly, one hand reaching out to brush lightly against her glowing cheeks. 'See? I'm real enough. Okay, okay, I'll get to the point, stop looking daggers at me.'

Impatiently, she brushed his hand away. 'You mean there *is* one?'

'Yes, indeed.' He sat up, serious again. 'You and I are going to do business together.'

'Business?'

'You're frowning.'

'What business?'

'I'm going to use your services, of course.'

'Oh!'

'Donna, dear, you're frowning even more now.'

'I'm . . . taken aback. What—what sort of function are you planning? How many people is it for? Where will it be?'

Daniel held up a hand. 'Don't get on your high horse. I'm talking about business in the future, I can't say exactly when, not just yet. But Kieren tells me you have to be booked well in advance because you're so damned good at what you do. That's why I want you and not someone else, before you ask. And you're still frowning. Dammit, I feared this would happen, this is why I wanted us to get to know one another a little, for you to get rid of this stupid resentment of me. But you're so stubborn, you're going to refuse even to do business with me, aren't you?'

'No.'

It was his turn to be taken aback.

'That's where you're wrong, Mr Conrad, absolutely wrong! Believe me, it'll be my pleasure to take money off you.'

'We-ll! This is most satisfactory, most satisfactory.' He glanced at his watch. 'We'll have to talk about it. I have to go now, so I'll pick you up at ten on Sunday. Don't keep me waiting, I can't bear unpunctuality. Dress casually, we'll have a picnic by the river, weather permitting. Now, can I escort you back to your shop?'

'I—but I——'

'Your mouth's opening and closing like that of a demented fish. A straight yes or no will do.'

'*No!*' She shouted the word loudly, unthinking. He had laid a trap and she had walked straight into it! Sunday. With him. There was no way she would get out of it now, not now she'd agreed to do business with him. She was like a fish—on the hook.

'Is anything wrong?' The head waiter had appeared in response to her shout.

'Everything's wrong,' Daniel said helplessly, dramatically. 'I just asked Miss Kent here to marry me but she didn't seem at all keen on the idea.'

With a glance of pure hatred at Daniel and an apologetic, half-hearted smile at the waiter, Donna excused herself and went back to work.

CHAPTER SEVEN

SHE was ready and waiting at ten on the dot on Sunday. Ready, waiting but unwilling. When the doorbell rang, she braced herself. This was going to be an awful day and she would get rid of him as soon as she possibly could. She couldn't spare him the afternoon, even if she wanted to. She had work to do.

'Good morning, Donna. How lovely you're looking!'

She bit on her cheeks, determined not to laugh. The top half of his body was obscured by the biggest bouquet of flowers she had ever seen. There were white roses, pink ones, red ones and yellow ones. All roses. Dozens of them. And he'd spoken from behind the bouquet, hadn't even set eyes on her yet!

'Come in, you idiot.' She turned away stifling her laughter as she walked into her living room.

'As charming as ever! Now let me look at you.'

She turned to him, her eyebrows raised in indignation. She was wearing a khaki-coloured trouser suit in cotton, a casual, good-quality outfit which had been one of her bargain finds—a snip at half the price.

'Can't say that colour does much for you,' Daniel said, as if his opinion mattered to her. 'Go and stick these in the sink.'

'I'll put them in vases——'

'You can do that later. Just a minute.' He fished into his jacket pocket and came out with—of all things—a pair of nail scissors. 'Come here, Donna.'

She looked at him askance. Unable to hold back her laughter this time, she gave vent to it. 'Daniel, are you absolutely clueless? You can't use nail scissors to cut down roses!' She was having the first good laugh she'd had in ages, her arms full of the cellophane-wrapped bouquet with it's big bow.

84

Daniel looked heavenward, took hold of her by the shoulders and turned her round so that she had her back to him, 'Keep still, this could be tricky.'

'What are you *doing*?' she squealed. She could feel him lifting her hair! Suddenly, it was released and she was being turned round again.

He stood, smiling, with what used to be an elastic band dangling from the fingers of one hand, the nail scissors dangling from the other. 'I came prepared,' he informed her, his smile broadening, lighting up his eyes.

Donna tossed her hair back. The man was incorrigible. 'You're hardly my idea of a boy scout,' she muttered on her way to the kitchen.

Many hours later, at midnight to be precise, she lay in her bed and thought again about the nail scissors, about Daniel's remark as she'd opened the door to him. No wonder she couldn't sleep, she kept on thinking about it and she kept on laughing. It seemed even funnier in retrospect.

Of course she was suspicious of him. She couldn't shake that feeling. He was making an effort to get to know her and it went beyond the realm of business. Was he up to something? But what could he be up to? No, no, she must stop being suspicious. He'd been right the previous week, when he'd accused her of still resenting him. It made no sense at all, but she did. Even now.

Yet she had had a lovely day with him. Somehow he'd talked her into having dinner with him—she wasn't quite sure how. The entire day had left her bemused, from the roses to the picnic hamper he'd brought, along with champagne in an ice-box, to the dinner they'd had at a quaint little inn full of copper and brass and the smell of home-cooking.

They had got back to her house at ten-thirty. She hadn't had to insist on being brought home at a reasonable time, Daniel had put up no argument. It had been clear to both of them that she was in danger of falling asleep from nine o'clock onwards. She had been so relaxed from around noon onwards, it was as though her batteries had been runnning down and down until she could hardly keep her eyes open. Maybe it would have done her good. Maybe she should take some time off work . . . just occasionally.

He had dropped her off at the house with a cheery 'Good night', and that had been that. He'd made no attempt to fix another date—appointment. She preferred the word appointment where he was concerned. Yet they hadn't spoken a word of business. They seemed to have talked about everything but. His house purchase was going ahead, she'd learned. Kieren Gardner would do the conveyancing and would be quick about it. Daniel reckoned to move in in about a month—which suited the vendors nicely.

Donna turned over in bed, determined to go to sleep or at least to think about something else. How come she was distracted by thoughts of Daniel when by rights she should be sleeping like a log, she was so tired?

'It's himself.' Siggy jerked his white-hatted head in the direction of the office. He'd been the one to answer the 'phone because Donna was up to her elbows in flour.

'Himself?'

'Genghis Khan,' came the dry reply. 'You know very well who I mean—the ape who carried you out of here over his shoulder last week.'

'You didn't do much to help, did you?'

Siggy stuck both his hands on his hips. 'What could I have done? You didn't expect me to tackle him, did you? Wouldn't that be like using a walnut to break open a sledgehammer?'

Donna laughed all the way to the office. It was Wednesday. In spite of herself, she had thought often about Daniel Conrad since Sunday. She wiped her hands on her apron and picked up the 'phone. 'Daniel? Sorry to keep you.'

'That's okay.' She could hear the warmth in the deep voice. A dark brown voice. He was smiling, she could tell. 'How's Mister Pastry? He didn't seem at all pleased when I gave him my name. I don't think he likes me.'

'Why, Daniel! I'm sure he thinks you're lovely.'

'Oh, God!'

'Relax, I'm lying. Besides, I didn't mean that. Behave yourself and leave my Siggy alone.'

She didn't catch his next words. The next thing she heard was, 'We've yet to talk business.'

'I know it.'

'I'd love to take you out to dinner tonight——'

'I'm doing a party.'

'But I can't because you're doing a party. How about tomorrow?'

'I'm doing a party.'

'And I'm going to one on Friday, alas. It's the shindig of a good customer so I'd better go. Would you care to be my escort?'

'Not a chance.'

'Work?'

She shook her head, as if he could see her. 'Lack of inclination. You didn't think I'd fall for that one, did you? We couldn't talk business if we were at a party.'

'No,' he agreed, his voice growing softer. 'But we could talk and laugh and dance and—if you're very good—maybe even smooch a little.'

'*Smooch?*' Donna held the receiver at arm's length, looking at it as if it were responsible for offending her. What kind of word was that? And the idea of it, smooching with Daniel Conrad! She couldn't even visualise herself dancing with him.

The receiver was laughing at her, deep, audacious laughter which had her biting her cheeks again. He was crazy, it was as simple as that. 'Daniel, I'm extremely busy and you're wasting my time.'

'I'll bet you've got that rubber band round your hair . . .'

'Daniel!'

'And now your eyes are getting darker because you're vexed . . .'

'*Daniel!*'

'Ah, well.' He sighed an exaggerated sigh. 'Then it'll have to be Sunday, I suppose. I'll pick you up at ten. Be ready.'

'But——'

But nothing. He'd hung up.

Donna put the 'phone down and stared at it. This was wrong, all of it. She shouldn't be doing it. She shouldn't be taking time off on Sundays, she shouldn't be seeing him, she shouldn't allow herself to be so amused by his sense of humour. Nor should she do business with him. She didn't need his business so why was she bothering? Because it entertained her, the idea of making a profit out of him?

She really wasn't sure.

'What did he want?' Siggy asked when she got back into the kitchen. 'You look cross.'

'I——' Did she? Siggy's question surprised her, so did his remark. 'No, I'm not cross. I've agreed to do business with Mr Conrad. He's Daniel Conrad, by the way, and—er—we're meeting on Sunday to talk about it.'

Siggy nodded, said nothing. It was by no means unusual for Donna to see customers on a Sunday.

'As a matter of fact . . .' She hesitated. Should she tell Siggy or not? 'I've—been out with him for the past couple of weekends. Sundays, that is. And last Sunday I spent the whole day with him.'

'And?' Siggy stopped what he was doing.

'And nothing. What do you mean?'

He shrugged expansively. 'I didn't ask, love, you volunteered. So tell me now whether that was a good thing for you or a bad thing. I'm not a mind reader.'

A good thing or a bad thing? She repeated the words to herself, pondering. 'Neither, I suppose. We've—sort of patched up our differences. I mean, I'd met him before, as you know and—hadn't got on at all well with him. But, yes, all in all I suppose it's a good thing. I enjoyed myself on Sunday,' she finished with a smile.

Siggy was positively beaming. 'Then I'll have to revise my opinion of the man. If he's making you happy instead of miserable or furious, I'm on his side. Anyone who can get you to take a day off work can't be bad!' And with that he put an arm around her shoulders and hugged her tightly.

July slipped into August and the weather continued to be extremely kind. It was a quiet month for Donna because so many people were away on holiday. She went out with Daniel every Sunday and, throughout the month, on several evenings during mid-week.

She told herself this would stop come September, when she was busier again, she told herself that he kept manipulating her into these dates, that he was a past master of persuasion. Then she would tell herself off for allowing him to manipulate her, admit to herself that she was in fact a willing victim because she liked his company. And she did, in spite of herself she liked his company very much, the laughter, the teasing, the serious conversations when they would talk over some subject or other and thrash out their differences of opinion.

Daniel was always stimulating, always entertaining. He always planned ahead so that their arrangements went smoothly, knowing exactly where he was taking her and how to get there. They went to some far-flung restaurants, places neither of them had been to before, and they went into London a few times, to a concert or a play or something very frivolous. It didn't make things easier, discovering that he was as catholic as she when it came to entertainment. He enjoyed, as she did, almost everything.

Of course she had tried to resist him, most especially when it came to mid-week dates, but he always came up with some reason why she shouldn't refuse, or cancel after an arrangement had been made. It had been, 'But, Donna, I've just collected our tickets! I was in London today and I went out of my way to make sure ...' There had also been, 'You can't change your mind,

that's just not on! Have you forgotten that Kieren's
coming with us? It's his birthday, remember? I've
booked a table for four, and you don't want to hurt
Kieren's feelings by opting out, do you?'

They had spent a couple of evenings with Kieren
Gardner and his girlfriend—two different girlfriends.
Those evenings had been fun, too.

It was when Kieren called in at the shop alone one
day that Donna was forced to acknowledge quite how
much of an effect Daniel was having on her life. The
law practice was in the same street as the pâtisserie and
it wasn't unusual for him to stick his head round the
office door, saying hello on the days he called in to buy
a sandwich or something.

On the last Friday of August, he came in and sat
himself down without being invited to. Donna was
doing the wages and the interruption was something she
could have lived without. Still, she had a ready smile for
him.

''Morning, Kieren, what can I do for you?'

This was met by a sardonic smile. 'You can satisfy
my curiosity.' He sat, watching her in amusement. 'You
know, I'm a good sport, Donna, it's no secret that I
fancy you, so I can't blame Dan for feeling the same
way.'

She stopped what she was doing, nonplussed. 'He
doesn't fancy me. I—we—we're just . . .'

While she faltered, wondering quite how to describe
her relationship with Kieren's friend, he folded his arms
and watched her, obviously highly amused. 'Yes,
Donna?'

'This is none of your business, actually.'

'True, true. But I'm curious. I mean, there's a male
ego involved in all this, you know. Mine. I can't help
wondering what old Daniel has that I haven't got.'

Donna couldn't explain that, either. Both men were
good-looking, successful . . . yet so different.

She wasn't going to be drawn into this, she found it
worrying and she didn't want to start analysing what

she was doing. This friendship with Daniel was only temporary, unimportant. 'Hop it, will you, Kieren? I've got so much to do, you wouldn't believe it.'

'I see.' He laughed, a good-natured laugh. 'I see you're as informative as Daniel, I can't get anything out of him, either.'

'That's because there's nothing to discover.'

'But—just tell me what your relationship was in the past. He's twelve years older than you, you're too young to have been his girlfriend.'

'What's he told you?'

'Nothing, I've just said I can't get anything out of him.'

Donna sighed, finding that she respected Daniel for this. He was still living with Kieren; the two men were friends of many years, yet Daniel had said nothing at all about . . . 'He was a—no, his father was a friend of my father's, at one time. They did business together and some socialising, not a great deal. My father was a builder and he bought timber and general supplies from Conrad's in Lincoln.'

'I see. You said "was". I take it your father's retired now?'

Feeling herself stiffen, she nodded. 'I suppose you could put it like that. He's dead, Kieren. Both my parents are dead. Daddy died in a road . . . accident. We're digressing,' she added quickly. 'You wanted to know what my relationship was with Daniel in the past. Well, there wasn't one. Before the night of your barbecue, I'd only met him twice. As for your male ego . . . don't feel bruised. To be honest, I don't quite know how Daniel keeps persuading me to spend time with him. I'm catering for this big office party of his in November, as you know, the official opening. It's good business for me . . . so shall we say I'm just keeping one of my customers sweet and leave it at that?'

Kieren's handsome face was wreathed in smiles. 'I'll leave it at that, pretty one, rubbish though it is. You never kept me sweet by coming out with me!'

There was no answer to that, either. To her chagrin, Donna felt colour rising in her cheeks. She was extremely grateful when Kieren promptly let her off the hook. He stood, reaching over to put a cool hand against her face. 'Okay, I'll bow out gracefully. Dammit!'

He laughed as he walked the short distance to the door. Then he turned round abruptly, as if he had just made up his mind about something. He looked troubled now. 'Donna, there's ... there's something I feel I ought to say. All joking aside, don't delude yourself. I got to know Daniel very well when we were at Oxford and I know the story of his life since then. I knew his wife, I know how much he loved her. You might regard his pursuit of you as a game or something, but it isn't. Dan's working like a maniac right now, I've seen little of him except for the foursomes we've had. He leaves for Uxbridge around seven in the morning and he's never back before midnight. I see that's news to you. Well, he's working like a dog to get the transport company established as he wants it. He's also got his house to sort out.

'Virtually the only time he has off is the time when he's with you. It's the same with you, isn't it? You're both crazy about work, which in my book means you're both crazy, full-stop. There's something driving the pair of you and, frankly, I find it worrying because I like you both very much. I care. It's because I care that ... well, the point I want to make is this: whatever you do, please take care not to hurt Dan. He's——'

'*Hurt* him?' She was incredulous. If she hadn't been so stunned, she would have laughed.

'I know, I know.' Kieren held up a hand. 'You think I'm reading too much into your friendship with him. But I'm not, Donna. It's over four years since his wife died and to my knowledge he's never taken out the same woman twice in all that time. I don't think he even glanced at a woman for the first two years after

Mandy's death and after that there've been only—you know.'

Donna nodded, listening intently to every word. 'A series of one night stands?'

'Quite. Infrequent ones at that. So you see, there's something special about you and I'm not the only one who thinks so.'

Kieren let himself out, leaving Donna in a state of bewilderment. She slumped forward as she sat, resting her chin on her hands. *Did* Daniel think her special? If so, why? She had given him no encouragement whatsoever. On the contrary. He had never made a pass at her, either. Now did that add to Kieren's theory or did it detract from it? Did Daniel regard her as a friend—and only a friend—or was he playing some sort of waiting game? If so, for what?

She was grateful to Kieren for having visited. She spent the next hour mulling things over; she had been forced to think. Surely there couldn't be even the slightest danger of Daniel falling in love with her? That was what Kieren had been getting at, wasn't it? When he had cautioned her not to hurt him.

Two months had passed since Kieren's barbecue, since her strange relationship with Daniel had begun. Two months in which so many things had happened very insidiously. It was time to take stock.

Donna did just that. When had she started to look forward to Sundays? When, exactly, had she made up her mind to shop for new clothes—clothes to wear on her dates with Daniel? At what point had she started to leave her hair loose permanently, except when she was cooking? On which date had she decided to invite him into her home afterwards, and sat with him till the early hours of the morning, talking and drinking endless cups of coffee?

So many things had sneaked up on her and, now, she was forced to ask herself what the devil she thought she was doing. The life she had had so very carefully under control had slipped a gear. She was no longer focusing one hundred per cent concentration on her business.

And this would not do.

She would tell Daniel tonight that she wasn't going to see him again. That was another thing—tonight—she had invited him to have dinner with her, at home, having thought it was high time she reciprocated all the dinners he'd bought her.

She must be getting soft.

On the other hand, perhaps it was just as well he was coming round tonight. She wanted to tell him straight away that it was over—whatever *it* was—so it was just as well she would be able to talk to him in private because she had a feeling he wouldn't take kindly to the news. And she knew from experience how wickedly he could behave in public. He was the sort of man who didn't give a damn what people thought of him.

CHAPTER EIGHT

DANIEL did not take kindly to the news. He took it quietly, though. To begin with he took it so quietly that Donna was convinced he hadn't heard her.

She had dashed home from work and done a quick rearrangement of the furniture in her living room, had put in there the small, folding table that lived in what should have been her dining room. She had set it with an immaculate linen table cloth and matching napkins, her best glassware and cutlery, then she'd prepared dinner, had a quick bath, got dressed, made-up and started cooking.

Daniel had arrived as punctually as ever, on the dot of eight, with an armful of roses and two bottles of wine, one red and one white. 'I didn't know what we'd be eating,' he'd said, 'so I covered all contingencies.'

'Did you hear me, Daniel?' She spoke to him almost sharply now, watching for a reaction. They were just finishing pudding, still sitting at the small table. 'I said after tonight I'm not seeing you any more.'

He kept on eating.

She tensed, at a loss to understand his silence. He wasn't even looking at her. 'I mean, I'll see you when we actually get down to planning the food for your party, obviously, but until then I . . . Dammit, have you heard one word of what I've just said to you?'

'I heard.'

'So?'

He finished the last of the food on his plate, pushed his chair back, stretched his legs and regarded her intently. 'So you still resent me. You disappoint me, Donna.'

She rarely saw him this serious, this intense. She felt

suddenly very awkward, self-conscious. 'Daniel, it *isn't* that. That doesn't make sense——'

'You're telling me, it doesn't. But it's there nevertheless. You just can't separate the past from the present. Even now, you're incapable of doing that. And the crazy thing is that I was innocent of your accusations in the past.'

'I know, I've told you I know that.'

'So what's this all about? If you really have got rid of your resentment of me, why stop seeing me? We have fun together, don't we? What's the harm in it?'

He was not, he absolutely was not going to talk her out of her decision. Not this time. She was determined about that. What she said next was the truth, she did not need to lie. Though he was taking this very quietly and calmly, he was angry, she could sense it. 'I'll tell you what it's all about, Daniel, you're a distraction.'

'I'm flattered.'

'Don't be sarcastic, please listen. I am very, very tired——'

'That makes two of us.'

'Daniel, please! Give me a chance, since you obviously feel I owe you an explanation. There simply isn't room in my life for anything, or anyone, except my business. I love it and I want to expand it. I've told you that before, you've even made some suggestions to me, for which I'm grateful. The thing is, August has been a comparatively quiet month for me so I have had some free time. I've been able to make time to go out. Towards the middle of September things will start picking up again and by October I'll be working flat out. The top and bottom of it is——'

'That you have no time for me.' He said it quietly, looking her straight in the eye.

She lifted her chin. 'Precisely.'

He didn't react. Again, she felt awkward. Something in her, somewhere, wanted him to put up an argument. There was none forthcoming. At the same time, part of her was relieved, the main part of her. It had been so easy. 'Shall I go and put the coffee on? Oh, I've got some Stilton, I almost forgot. It's absolutely perfect, shall we have some?'

'I'd love some, thanks.' He smiled at her, a warm and friendly smile which reached his eyes. 'That was a superb meal, by the way, I'm sorry it turned out to be a farewell dinner.'

Donna stood in the kitchen for a minute or more without even moving. She was horrified to find that her hands were trembling. It had been so easy, why was she feeling disappointed? In whom was she disappointed, herself or the man in the other room? She put the coffee on and got out the cheese and biscuits while waiting for it to perc.

'Oh, my God! *Daniel!*'

He was with her in a flash, finding her white-faced, clutching at the worktop with her right hand while blood spurted from the index finger of her left.

Daniel's arm went rapidly around her waist and she leaned heavily against him, sure she was about to faint. 'Take it easy,' he murmured. 'How did you manage to do that?'

'I can't stand the sight of blood! I don't—I couldn't find my cheese knife so I used the bread knife and—oh, Lord, it's going to need a stitch, isn't it? I hate hospitals!'

'I'll tell you in a minute. Come over to the sink.' Keeping one arm firmly around her, he took hold of her hand and stuck it under the cold water tap. He had a second or two to inspect the cut before it was covered in blood again. 'No, it'll be okay. It's quite deep but it's very small. It'll knit together. Where can I find a plaster?'

'In the bathroom cabinet.' She was beginning to feel idiotic. So much fuss over such a small cut; she couldn't even feel anything, if only it would stop bleeding so ...

'Stay where you are, my lovely. Hold on to the sink and I'll be back in a jiff.'

He was back in seconds, but not before she had felt

the tears at the back of her eyes. He was, really, a lovely person, kind and thoughtful and generous. He was as calm as anything now, just what she needed. But she mustn't weaken, she must stick to her decision.

Ten minutes later she was cleaned up, patched up and drinking coffee. They didn't bother with the cheese. Daniel had made her sit down because she was trembling, had seen to the coffee himself and insisted she have some brandy.

'All right, Donna? You're very white, not still in danger of fainting, are you?'

'No. I—oh, Daniel, I'm so *tired*! I don't know what's wrong with me lately. I've done less work than usual but I'm more tired than ever. Do you think I'm anaemic or something? I mean, I can't imagine what else it can be—though I eat sensibly, take a balanced diet, as you know.'

'Poor Donna,' he said quietly. 'You're really quite blind to some things, aren't you? Don't you know where you're heading? One of these days you're going to collapse and you won't get up again for six months. Enforced rest, they call it. I know because it happened to me.'

'What? What do you mean?' She stared at him across the small distance in her living room. He was sitting on her settee, the two-seater which diminished in size when he was occupying it.

'Not the collapse, I don't mean that. I mean the syndrome, the work syndrome. It becomes an obsession, doesn't it? Until the day you learn that work is not what life's all about.'

'But—you've lost me. No one works harder than you do. Kieren's told me about the hours you're putting in. He told me the night I met you that you're a workaholic. I think he worries about you.'

'Then he's worrying needlessly, he's out of date. Believe me, the pace I'm going at just now is only temporary. That is, it's the end of four years of . . . I don't know what to call it. Compulsive obsession, perhaps.'

Donna held her breath. Four years, he'd said. 'The four years since your wife died, Daniel?'

'Yes,' he said quietly. 'Here,' he fished in his pocket and pulled out a set of keys. 'Catch!'

'What . . . I don't understand. What are these?'

'I have a house in Sardinia. Have I mentioned that to you? No? Well, I suppose I should describe it as a villa. It's quite a distance from its nearest neighbour and has a stretch of private beach in front of it. There's a maid who goes in regularly to check that everything's okay and who looks after any friends of mine who go over for holidays. There's nobody there now. Why don't you go there for a while, Donna? For heaven's sake give yourself a good rest before it's forced upon you.'

'That's impossible. But thanks, it's very nice of you.' She was about to throw the keys back but he signalled her not to.

'No, keep them, I have another set. I brought those with me tonight because you'd told me your diary's clear for the next week or so. Just hold on to them and use them when you want to. Note my choice of words, Donna, when you want to. Right now you're making excuses. You could go, take at least a week, but you won't because you simply don't want to. There's nothing pressing right now, nothing Siggy couldn't handle, but you simply don't want to take a rest. You see, I know you rather well, I've been watching you for weeks. I know how shattered you are, it's the result of six years of maniacal work, non-stop work.

'You've been enjoying yourself with me, yet you want to put an end to it. I've watched your face when we've been doing the simplest of things—like that musical we went to last week. You loved it. You've lived all these years in Richmond and not once, you said, had you been to a West End theatre. I found that incredible, especially in one who loves the theatre. So come on, Donna,' he finished softly, his eyes so gentle on her that she was almost mesmerised by them, 'tell me what it's all about, this evening, this decision and this obsession of yours. Why are you punishing yourself? Why, Donna?'

'Punishing myself? I'm not punishing myself, I'm just ambitious, that's all.'

'No, there's more to it than that, as was the case with me. I worked like a fool for four solid years because after my wife's death it was the only way I could cope with my loneliness. There was also, initially, a great deal of anger in me because Mandy had been taken so young. She was twenty-nine when she died. After that, there was . . . nothing. Nothing at all. At least that's how it seemed for a long time. We would have had children, we wanted to but . . . Mandy's illness was diagnosed just five months after we got married. For the following nineteen months she went through hell with all sorts of treatments. She was a brave girl but none of them worked.'

He looked down at his hands, quiet for a moment before bringing his eyes back to hers. 'I threw myself into my work as a means of escape, and that's a lot more compulsive than mere ambition. In time the pain faded and the day came when I realised there was more to life than work. That's when I bought the house in Sardinia, just ten months ago. I spent some time alone there and decided I had to sort myself out, settle somewhere different and start building a life outside of work. Once I've got this company on its feet I'm going to take life much more easily, very much more. I'm over Mandy's death and I'm ready to live again, to love again. To marry again, if I'm lucky. I no longer need to work myself into the ground to stop myself from thinking, to stop myself from being myself.'

Confused, Donna regarded him suspiciously. 'What are you getting at, Daniel?'

His eyes moved to the wedding photograph of her parents, which stood on the mantelpiece. 'You. It's all tied up with him, your so-called ambition, your obsession with work. It's all tied up with your father, with your thinking he committed suicide. You can't get over it. This is what's preventing *you* from living like a normal human being, it's giving you a sense of inadequacy, a sense of worthlessness.'

'Rubbish!' She waved his words away, they weren't even worth considering.

'Think about it. You told me how much it hurts, that you weren't enough for him to live for. *Hurts*, Donna. Present tense. It's still eating away at you and the pity of it is that you're wrong. *Wrong*. Your father's death was accidental.'

'I don't believe that. You don't know that, you can't know it. He was a wonderful driver. He was altogether a marvellous man. He ... just gave up on life,' she added lamely. 'I don't think he'd got over Mummy's death, apart from ... his other troubles.'

Daniel's eyes closed. He wanted to tell her, God how he wanted to tell her he knew without doubt that Joseph Kent had not taken his own life. He had wanted to tell her a dozen times before. And still he could not, not yet. It would necessitate telling her *how* he knew, and she wouldn't be able to handle that, most especially coming from him. Even now, she was getting angry.

'Daniel, are you listening to me? I said I want you to go now.'

'Of course you want me to go,' he said quietly, 'because I've been telling you a few home truths and the truth hurts sometimes, doesn't it?'

'You haven't hurt me,' she snapped. 'You're not capable of doing that, don't flatter yourself. You've been talking nonsense, Daniel. I don't feel inadequate, far from it! I've done very well for myself considering I started out with nothing. As for——'

'You have,' he cut in. 'I agree.' He opened his eyes, letting her see that he meant what he said. 'I admire you, Donna, I really do, especially when I remind myself that you're only twenty-four years old.'

'So what are you going on about?'

'Precisely that. You are young, but you're not all that young. You've been working seven days a week and most evenings since you were eighteen and making cakes for people in your spare time. You've had no youth, your life's still empty and presumably celibate and one of these days you're going to wake up and find you're forty years old. And believe me, you'll ask yourself then, where have all those years gone? Where was the laughter, the sunshine, the love? Don't let that happen, Donna.' He held her gaze, his eyes intent upon her. 'Because all the money in the world can't buy those things.'

Not knowing quite what to say, she said nothing at all.

'Would you mind telling me,' he asked gently, 'what it is you're trying to prove? And to whom?'

Had he couched the question in a sarcastic or clever way, she'd have thrown him out there and then. Had he given the impression that he *expected* her to answer, she'd have said it was none of his business. But he hadn't done either of these things. He had looked at her with unmistakable concern, genuine interest, and so she told him the truth.

'My ultimate ambition is to go back to live in my house in the Wolds. You know how beautiful it is there, how lovely the house is. My roots are there, that's where I want to be. As soon as I can afford it. I've no intention of working at this pace forever, just for a few more years. I'm going to form a limited company, get bigger premises. If I had twice the kitchen scope and more storage space—well, I've told you quite a bit about that. The business is here for the taking, I could double my turnover easily if I had more space, more staff, if I delegate and leave myself free to concentrate on promoting the company.'

Daniel was staring at her. 'You still haven't answered my question, Donna.'

Nor had she. 'I was getting to that. All right.' She got up, too irritated to remain seated. 'I suppose I am trying to prove myself capable, to prove I'm not a quitter, but it isn't wholly for me, it's to show all those people in Lincolnshire, all those who did the gossiping.'

'What gossiping?' he asked quickly, a little too quickly.

'Oh, come on! You must have heard it, you were a part of it. I can't quote specifics to you, I can only tell you that when I went home during the summer, after Daddy's funeral, there was a great deal of nudging and shaking of heads in the village. When I went shopping. Some people crossed over to the other side of the street to avoid me! A few actually *snubbed me*. And these people I'd known all my life! I can't tell you how *angry* that made me, still makes me! I feel as if there's a stigma attached to my name.'

'A stigma? There's no stigma! That's all in your mind.'

'No, it isn't. So to answer your question fully, it's partly a matter of pride, I'll admit that. One day I'm going back to show them all!'

'Show them all?' Daniel was incredulous. 'Who? Who do you think gives a damn about anything, six years on? And what are these people to you? Nothing! Gossips, one-time neighbours, that's all. The person you were most angry with is sitting right here with you now—and you've already shown me what you're made of. I've just told you I admire you. Isn't that enough?'

He got rapidly to his feet, grabbing hold of her by the shoulders and shaking her. 'Donna, all of this is nonsense. Oh, I know it's what you feel like doing but you're so mixed up, so twisted in your thinking, you can't see straight. Common sense is playing no part in it. You're working like a demon and missing out on the best years of your life—for what? So you can go back to the Wolds and live like a hermit in that big house, just because you're too stubborn to let it go? Or so you can show a bunch of unimportant people that you're a worthwhile person and a success? People who mean nothing to you, people who don't give a damn by now, if they ever did.

'Are you completely mad? What do you think you're going to do there, once you're back in your precious house, back in the past? Are you going to have so much money that you'll be able to live off your capital? Will you be happy then? As what—as a comfortable old maid? A successful, proud, I've-shown-them-all, lonely old maid? Is that what all your plans are leading you to?'

'Let go of me!' She wrenched away from him. 'No, of course not! Don't be ridiculous. I'll run my business from my house, I'll——!'

'Donna, *think*! Sit yourself down sometime and think about all this. I've never heard anything so idiotic! You're messing up your life, fixing your sights on some ludicrous goal and it's *all* because you think your beloved, "marvellous" father killed himself.' He caught hold of her again, his fingers closing tightly on her upper arm. 'That *is* what's at the root of all this, this muddled thinking of yours!'

'Don't you dare speak of my father in that tone. Let *go* of me!'

'When I'm ready, you idiot girl.' His voice was quiet in contrast to hers. He was as angry as she but unlike her, he was in control of himself. 'You've got a flourishing, successful, well-established business here in the south—and you plan one day to up-sticks and move back into the past, to start all over again. To start scouting for business and building a reputation all over again, to go back to square one. I mean, I have understood you correctly? This is what you're telling me? For *what*?'

He let go of her abruptly, turning away and running his fingers impatiently through his hair. 'The daftest thing of all is that somewhere inside your mind, you know as well as I do that you'll never carry out these plans of yours. They're just based on emotion, they're nonsensical, just dreams of something you think you're going to do in the future. At X point in the future. Yet you know you'll never do it because you *know*, basically, that it makes no sense. Let go of the idea,

Donna. Make money, by all means, if that's what you want to do. But do it to please yourself. You don't need an excuse, you don't need to prove anything to anyone. If you must miss out on life and work yourself into the ground, at least be honest as to your motives.'

She was shaking her head, trying not to listen. He was upsetting her now as much as he'd upset her in the past. 'Get out of here, Daniel. I don't want to hear all this. It has nothing to do with you.'

'I wish I could believe that. *Let go of the past, Donna.* Get rid of that house. Take the money and use it to expand your business here, if you're really set on making a lot of money. Doesn't that make more sense than taking your business to the house?'

'Get out,' she shouted. 'I don't want to see you again, ever. Get out of my life and stop interfering!'

'I'm going,' he said curtly. 'You will think over all I've said. You won't be able not to. And remember what I said about all the things money can't buy.'

'Go, Daniel, *go*! You're more than a distraction, you're disturbing me.' She was nearly crying, she felt as if the very purpose of her existence was being threatened by the things he'd said.

'Donna——' He caught hold of her swiftly, pulling her towards him.

Suddenly she felt the length of his body against hers and the shock of it made her go rigid as his arms closed tightly around her waist. He looked down at her, reaching one hand to brush lightly over her cheek. Quietly, calmly, he said, 'You're a disturbance to me, too. A pleasant one. Why do you think I want your company, Donna, because I'm out to upset you? Do you think my life's ambition is to bring ruin and unhappiness to people whose name is Kent?'

'No, I——' She looked away, feeling lightheaded, aware of the warmth of his body through the thin material of her dress. Her heart was beating wildly as she stood, wanting to pull away from him yet unable to move.

'Look at me, Donna.'

She dragged her eyes back to his, knowing he was about to kiss her. Her eyes widened with something approaching fear. She could hardly breathe, her heart seemed to be beating in her throat.

'No,' he said softly, his eyes laughing at her. 'You're in no danger of being kissed.' He put her away from him, holding her at arm's length. 'If I kissed you now it would only add to your confusion. And I don't play unfairly, believe it or not.'

She didn't know what he meant, nor did she know how he had read her mind. She didn't know either why she wanted desperately for him to kiss her before they parted, as part they must. She had no idea how this man had manoeuvred his way into her life, she knew only that she had to get him out of it.

'Ring me,' he was saying. 'When you want to, when you're ready to. I'll be moving into my house in a few days, as soon as I get a bed in there. You've got my 'phone numbers. Ring me anywhere, any time, whenever you want.'

She stepped away from him, breaking all physical contact. 'I shan't be ringing you, Daniel. I'm not going to do your party, you can get someone else. There are other caterers around.'

'I wasn't referring to the party. I was saying you can ring me any time, any time you want a friend to talk to. Remember there are no strings, I am on your side.'

CHAPTER NINE

A WEEK went by. Donna cried a lot during that week, at night, in bed, when her mind would go round and round with thoughts and emotions which made no sense to her. She told herself over and over that getting rid of Daniel was the best thing she could have done. Yet she missed him. Suddenly there was nothing to look forward to anymore.

There wasn't even her dream to look forward to. He had shattered that for her. He had been right in telling her she would be unable to avoid thinking over all he'd said. She couldn't stop thinking about it. He'd also been right in saying that her dream was unrealistic and nonsensical, that somewhere inside her she knew that. She did. Really, she had known it for quite some time, since she had become well-established here in Richmond. It didn't make any sense to go back to Lincolnshire to have to start all over again. It had taken her six years to get where she was today, it would take another six years in the north. It was crazy; Daniel had been right.

Oh, but she resented having it spelt out for her! She hated him for forcing her into realism. He had taken away from her something that had pulsed through her, something which had kept her going, given her strength. And now she was forced to ask herself what it was all about, really? Money in itself had never been her motivation. She enjoyed her home comforts, her car, her clothes, but she had all that. She could sell her house in the Wolds and invest the money. It would have increased considerably in value during the past six years. She could invest the money and have financial security. She didn't need to expand her business.

Then there would be her moments of anger, anger

instead of tears. What right had Daniel had to step into
her life the way he had? How could she have allowed
that to happen? How could she have allowed him to get
at her like this, to confuse her so? She wished she'd
never set eyes on him, wished she had never done that
barbecue for Kieren.

Why did she miss Daniel? Why did she want to see
him again, when it would only lead to more frustration
for her? Why had she sat in her office at home, last
Sunday morning, staring like a fool at nothing? She had
looked out at the street below as if expecting his car to
pull up, she had even half-hoped that it would. She had
looked up at the sun, then down into the street, and
asked herself whether she really were a little mad. She
had worked all afternoon, having given up on the idea
of his coming. She had missed all the sunshine.

She did the same thing on the following Sunday, too,
after another week had passed. She had never actually
felt lonely before, why was she feeling that way now? It
rained on that Sunday. It rained solidly, all day. Yet she
still looked down at the street all morning, thinking that
Daniel would have known what to do with the day,
would have dreamt up something fun to do. The rain
wouldn't have bothered him. During the afternoon, she
worked. During the evening, she worked. She worked
until she couldn't keep her eyes open any longer. She
went to bed exhausted but unable to sleep. In her head
she could hear Daniel's words and she cursed him for
them. She had, that day, missed all the laughter.

'What's wrong with you, Donna?' Siggy flopped into a
chair and lit a cigarette. 'We're all making allowances,
you know, it's pretty obvious that you're not well, but
you can't go on treating people like this.'

'What?' Donna looked at him, having no idea what
he was talking about. 'Like what? And I'm very well,
there's nothing wrong with me!'

Siggy fixed her with his light blue gaze. His eyes were
sad. 'You've just upset Una.' He jerked his head in the

direction of the kitchen. 'She's in there crying. You bawled at her and she'd told you yesterday she'd be an hour late this morning, that she was going to the dentist's. Besides,' he waved a hand before she could answer, 'since when do you start panicking about getting things ready? That's my prerogative. I'm the temperamental chef.'

He tried to make a joke of it, to make his point without getting too heavy, but Donna was horrified. He was right. She had been snappy lately. 'Stay here, Siggy, I want to talk to you. I'll be back in a moment.'

She went into the kitchen and placated Una, who was a good worker and much appreciated. Donna told her just that and she apologised profusely. Five minutes later she was back in her smoke-filled office. 'Siggy, I ...' she sighed heavily, shaking her head. 'I don't really know what's wrong with me. I'm—very confused at the moment. Could you ... could you stand it if I cried on your shoulder? I need——' She broke off, her eyes suddenly filling with tears which spilled over. She had been about to say that she needed a friend to talk to. Daniel had said he was her friend, had invited her to talk to him any time she wanted to. But she couldn't. It didn't feel right, thinking of him as a friend. Besides, all this had too much to do with him. She needed an independent ear, an objective one.

'I need a friend, Siggy. I can't talk to Kieren Gardner because he's—he's——'

'A friend of Daniel Conrad.' Siggy nodded, his heart going out to her. There was going to be a shift in their relationship but he was equal to it. He had to listen and he had to help her if he could. She was precious to him. 'Go on, love. Tell Siggy. Have you fallen in love with the big ape? Is that it?'

'Oh, for God's sake!' Donna snapped at him, sniffing her tears away furiously. 'If you're going to be ridiculous about this, I can't talk to you at all!'

So that's how it was. Siggy sighed inwardly, frightened for her. Since Daniel Conrad had appeared on the scene, Siggy had watched Donna changing. Over the weeks, she had softened, she had become ... feminine ... and as a result of it prettier than ever. Her way of dressing had changed, she'd started to smile more often than she used to, she laughed easily. To put it simply, she had been happier.

But the past two weeks had seen an end to that, they had been almost disastrous. She was snappy, tense, she had a haunted look about her and it was all due to Daniel. Daniel's absence. Daniel's being off the scene. There had been no 'phone calls from him for over a fortnight.

'Sorry, love,' he said quietly. 'My mistake.' He looked at her, shrugging. 'Why don't you tell me all about it, Donna? I mean everything.'

'I want to,' she said helplessly. 'But it's impractical here. Will you come to my house tonight? Can we talk then?'

'You bet.' Siggy crushed out his cigarette and got up. 'I'll be there on the dot of seven. I'll cook you a nice meal and then we'll talk.'

Everything. She talked to Siggy that evening and she told him every single detail of her story, from the moment she'd got the news of her father's death whilst at catering college to all the things Daniel had said to her when last they'd seen one another.

At length, Siggy looked at her tentatively. She wasn't going to like what he was about to say.

'Go on,' she said, 'tell me what you think. Be truthful, please.'

He nodded, his eyes going to the photograph on her mantelpiece. 'I don't think it matters how your father died. I think——'

'Siggy!'

'I think it's high time you accepted what you yourself once said to Daniel, that nothing can be changed. Daddy's dead, gone. You've got to forgive him for dying.'

'Forgive ... I don't understand.'

'I mean that Daniel's right in my opinion. This suicide idea is the root of your trouble, it is making you feel inadequate, as though you're not good enough to love. I've wondered myself what drives you so, and it's this. You were eighteen and nothing much, just a kid. At least, that's what you thought at the time, or it's what you've talked yourself into thinking since. Even if it were suicide, it doesn't mean your father didn't love you. Maybe he'd just had a bellyful, got sick of living. And if it wasn't suicide, well, Daniel is right again, it means it was an accident and it had nothing whatever to do with you and your not being enough for him to live for. Do you see what I mean when I say it doesn't matter how he died?'

'No! I——'

'But you do, love. Think about it. Pick up that photo and look at your dad and tell him you forgive him for dying—however he died.'

There was a silence.

'Is that it?' she asked at length. 'Is that all you have to say?'

'No, not quite. I think the next thing you should do is go back to Lincolnshire. Go and visit your house, see how you feel about the place now. It'll cure you.'

'Cure me?'

'Of the past. You'll find that nothing will be the same. You can never go back, not after such a long time, and find things unchanged. Everything will be different, no matter how familiar, because you are different now. You've lived six years, you're that much older, that much different. Do it, Donna, go this weekend. First thing in the morning. I can cope without you at the shop.'

'No.' She looked away, almost resenting Siggy for saying what he'd said, for agreeing so much with Daniel. Of course that was unfair, she'd invited his opinion, had needed it. Nevertheless, they were wrong, both of them. 'Siggy, I ... I feel scared right now. I—

feel that if I let go of my dream, my ambition, I . . . I don't really know what life's all about.'

'Who does?' he asked. But he knew a damn sight more about life than she did, poor kid. He was twice her age and he'd had twice the pain, twice the pleasure, twice the time in which to ask himself all the big questions, the heavy questions. He knew what he wanted from life, and it wasn't much. She had to decide for herself what she wanted. Choosing his words with care, he added, 'Maybe Daniel had a point—about life—when he talked to you of laughter and sunshine and years that can't be recaptured. He sounds okay to me, Donna, and you know, even if you are a little in love with him, you could do a lot worse.'

She didn't snap this time. She just stared at Siggy and gave a little thought to the possibility. Could she be? Could she be just a little in love with Daniel? Her eyes moved to the photograph and she found herself feeling guilty, feeling as if she were being disloyal to her father by even considering the possibility. She shook her head, dismissing the notion entirely. It was too ridiculous.

Siggy got up then. There was no more he could say, no more he could say that would help her. He felt sad and very sorry for her, there was a terrible battle going on inside her and only she could resolve it. She, and time. What would be would be.

Fate stepped in. In the post the very next morning, Saturday, there was a letter from Donna's agents in Lincolnshire. The family who was currently living in her house wanted to buy it. She stared at the letter and read it over and over again, knowing it was weird that at this particular moment she should get a letter containing an offer of a very substantial sum of money for her home.

She answered the letter immediately, before leaving for work.

CHAPTER TEN

'KIEREN! How lovely to see you! Come in, come in. When did you get back? Have you had a good holiday? You've obviously had good weather.'

'Super.' Kieren glanced at her desk, she didn't seem to be doing much. 'Hey, if you've an hour to spare, why don't we go out for lunch? I came in for a sandwich but I'll scrap that idea. Anything to get an hour alone with you.'

Donna was in fact pressed for time. She was catering for a children's party that afternoon—which wasn't thrilling Siggy in the least, to put it mildly. It wasn't that he disliked children, it was that he had had to cancel his plans. He'd intended to go into London around five, he'd said. Now he was having to go with Donna to do the honours because Una was off, looking after her sick husband, and their part-time waitresses were rarely available during the day. Most of them had day jobs and worked for Donna in the evenings for extra money. 'I—yes, why not?'

Kieren grinned. He didn't think this was Christmas and his birthday all rolled into one, he knew why she was accepting his invitation. Alas and alack.

Donna picked up her jacket, feeling guilty. She was accepting Kieren's offer of lunch solely because she wanted to hear news of Daniel. Not that she would ask. But Kieren was bound to tell her something of him, bound to mention him.

It was the middle of October and it had been six weeks since she had said goodbye to Daniel. Six weeks, and she had not heard a word from him. He hadn't 'phoned, he had not tried to contact her in any way. She felt almost stupid because the chances were that he had forgotten her existence . . . yet she had lived through

those six weeks in a state of—of ambivalence as far as
he was concerned. He had been constantly in her mind.
She had cursed him and pined for him alternately,
sometimes simultaneously. It wasn't that she was in
love with him, far from that, it was just that he was
somehow under her skin. She did not quite know how
to describe the effect he had had on her, still had on
her, even to herself. A part of her longed to hear his
voice, see his face, look into those fascinating eyes of
his again. The other part of her dreaded the very idea of
that, all of it. Any of it.

Kieren did not mention his name. They went to the
Italian restaurant where she had sat with Daniel a few
months ago, and he told her about his holiday in
Jamaica, about the weather, about the hotel he'd stayed
in, about the girl he had taken with him, but he did not
mention Daniel's name once. He was waiting for
Donna to do that.

When Kieren made noises about having to get back
to the office, Donna could stand it no longer. Very
casually, she said, 'Yes, I have to get back, too. I've got
a children's party on this afternoon but I did want to
ask—er—how Daniel's getting on. Is he . . . is he okay?
I mean——'

Kieren smiled. 'He's fine. 'Course I've been away for
the past three weeks so I don't know quite what he's up
to. I mean, I haven't been to see his house yet.'

Nor had she. She had never seen the place. 'I—oh. I
suppose he's working as hard as ever?'

'Well, I 'phoned him last night, when I got back. He
sounded fine, as I say, and he says that everything's
going just great at work. He's got himself and his staff
organised very well. Typical, of course. He's . . . Donna,
why the hell don't you ring him yourself?'

She looked up, one hand fiddling with the handle of
her coffee cup. 'It's—I—don't feel inclined to,' she lied.
'It's only that I was wondering——'

'Whether he asked about you? No, he didn't. Look,
Donna, I don't know what's gone on between you,

honestly. All I know is that there's—what shall I say,
unfinished business between you? Ring him, for God's
sake, because I'll tell you this much: he won't ring you.
Not if it's you who said goodbye to him.'

'What—does that mean, exactly? I said goodbye to
him a dozen times in the beginning but he took no
notice. Why is he taking no for an answer now, all of a
sudden?'

'Because he obviously thought you meant it this time,
you twit. Ring him, Donna.'

'But I meant it before! I——'

'Look, I have to go.' Kieren looked at her
apologetically. 'Sorry, but I've got a client coming in at
two.'

Donna went back to her office with a heavy heart.
Kieren Gardner had been no help at all.

She 'phoned Daniel on the following Sunday, when
she found herself looking down into the street again,
when she realised she'd been sitting by the window for
almost two hours, staring out, doing nothing. There
was plenty she could have been doing, should have been
doing, but right then none of it seemed important. And
she had the perfect excuse to ring him.

She dialled his home number with trembling hands,
she knew it off by heart though she had never even been
to the house.

It rang and rang and she was just about to hang up
when he answered. 'Daniel?' She tightened her grip on
the receiver, hoping she could stick to the speech she'd
rehearsed.

He responded to her as if they had seen one another
only yesterday. 'Hello, Donna, how're things? Sorry
about that, I was in the bath.'

'Oh, I—er—I can ring back later.'

'No, that's okay.' Daniel stifled a smile. He'd begun
to think she would never ring, had begun to think he
should have kissed her, after all. He wanted to laugh
aloud with relief.

'I've—just been going through my diary,' Donna

went on jerkily. 'And your name's still written in for next month. The—the thing is, I was wondering——'

'Thank goodness for that!' Daniel interrupted her, wanting to make this easier for her. 'I'm in a fix, Donna, I need you. I've been so busy, I clean forgot about the opening party and by the time I tried to book another caterer—two, actually—I was told I was too late, they were booked on that particular date. I suppose with it being a Friday . . . is there any chance of your coming here now to discuss it?'

'Well, I——'

'I'd be very grateful. You see, this is my only chance, today. I'm going to be out of town for a couple of weeks from tomorrow.'

Disappointment and elation battled for precedence inside her. She could see him, would see him, today. Today! But then he was going away for a couple of weeks . . . and in any case, he might not want to see her again until the night of his party.

'Can you find your way to Chertsey?'

'Of course I can, you idiot.'

'Why, Donna! What a charming way to speak to your customers.' He closed his eyes. God, it was good to hear her voice. He gave her detailed directions for finding his house, hung up and finished drying himself.

Donna put the 'phone down, wondering what clothes she should change into. Oh, it had been so good to hear his voice! Perhaps the blue suit, the one she had bought a few weeks ago? Daniel had never seen her in it.

She dressed and made up with care, as nervous as any young girl about to keep her first date. She hated herself for feeling like that, for being so affected by the prospect of seeing him. She picked up her brush and attacked her hair with vigour, looking in the mirror and seeing it fall, pale blonde and loose around her shoulders. Then, as if in an act of defiance—against whom, she couldn't be sure, herself or Daniel—she gathered it into a ponytail clip on the crown of her head, twisted it around and pinned it into place.

His house was tricky to find. Donna drove down numerous country lanes and stopped twice to ask directions. Oh, but it was beautiful, the area in which he was living! It was quiet and picturesque; the autumn leaves were falling and the driveway to Daniel's house was a carpet of rust and red and gold.

She stopped her car halfway up the sweeping drive and paused to look at the house from some distance. It was big, far too big for one person. But then he could afford a place such as this easily, had probably always lived in a spacious home. It was built from dark red brick, a wide, no fuss sort of building with a gravel drive that appeared to go all the way round it. Lawns stretched from the side of the drive, with trees and bushes dotted here and there. If it were her place, she thought, she would have some flower beds put in, rose beds. All roses. There was such potential here, the grounds were gorgeous now but there was so much more that could be done with them! And was that an orchard she could see? To the right of the house, at the back?

Looking forward to seeing the house itself, she moved on, pulling up in front of the light oak door which swung open as she stepped out of her car. Donna froze momentarily, keeping her hand on the car to support herself. She felt suddenly weak; it seemed like far more than six weeks had passed since she had last looked at Daniel Conrad.

And there he was, framed in the doorway, tall and broad and good-looking, smiling in such a way that her heart started to accelerate all over again. He had such a strong face, with lean but rugged features, white, even teeth and a mouth which was nothing short of sensuous. She had never noticed that before, the sensuality there.

He was wearing plain grey slacks and a red, roll-neck sweater which fitted closely, hinting at the muscles of his chest, his flat stomach. There was no excess weight on this man, he was, simply, big. She approached him almost cautiously, returning his smile a little nervously, clutching her handbag and numerous folders in her arms.

'Good morning, Daniel. Or is it afternoon?'

'It's lunch-time,' he informed her, his eyes travelling slowly over her from top to bottom. 'I hope you haven't eaten, because I'm starving!'

'I——' She looked up at him. He was blocking the doorway, looking at her now with frank disapproval. 'What's the matter? Aren't you going to invite me in?'

'Have you brought your poisoned darts?' he asked, pointing a finger in the general direction of her head.

'What?'

'You look like a pygmy, Donna. What the devil have you done to your hair? It looks worse than I've ever seen it!'

Why was she laughing? Why was she standing here, listening to his insults and laughing as though she didn't give a damn what he thought of her! She just looked at him, laughing like an idiot, her blue eyes telling him it was good to see him again.

Daniel was laughing, too, and he voiced his thoughts. 'It's good to see you, too! Come in, come in. Here, let me take those folders off you.'

She handed him the folders and followed him into a square, spacious hall which was absolutely empty. There wasn't even a covering on the floor. It was parquet, showing the care that had gone into the polishing of it though it was covered with a layer of dust. 'Not got yourself sorted out yet, I see? Or is it just the hall you haven't got round to?'

'Oh, dear.' Daniel turned to look at her, shaking his head. 'If you expected the inside to look as good as the outside, you're in for a shock. I haven't got round to anything yet.'

Within half an hour, Donna realised that he meant what he said. She walked round the house with him, from empty room to empty room. There were five bedrooms, two very big ones with en suite bathrooms and built-in wardrobes. A third bathroom was next to the smallest bedroom and the only furniture on the entire upper floor was that of a bed in the master suite. There was nothing else at all.

It was the same on the ground floor, apart from a solitary settee and one coffee table in the living room, which was some forty feet long and twenty feet wide.

'Oh, Daniel!' Donna stood in the centre of it and looked around. 'What a gorgeous living room! Look at those huge windows!' The windows were in fact sliding doors which overlooked the gardens at the back of the house. She had been right about the orchard, she could see it now. And there was a tennis court, too, off to the left. 'It has such potential! Just think what you can do with a room this size. Why on earth haven't you started on it yet?'

A smile tugged at the corners of his mouth, though he was shaking his head wearily. How beautiful she looked, standing by the window, her face lit with enthusiasm, the autumn sun streaming in and catching the myriad golden glints in her hair. 'Because I need some guidance,' he said heavily. 'Come on, you've yet to see the kitchen. That's one room I think you'll approve of. The previous owners had it revamped completely about a year ago.'

It was a dream kitchen. At least, that's how Donna saw it. It was tiled from floor to ceiling, it was vast and behind the dozens of cupboards, or what appeared to be cupboards, there was everything any woman could want. Everything matched, the façade of the refrigerator, the washing machine and tumble dryer, the dishwasher, the doors which opened to reveal drawers, storage space, shelves. In the spotless, stainless steel sink unit there was a garbage disposal unit. There was a micro-wave oven, a split-level gas cooker—everything. 'Oh, wow! This is marvellous, Daniel!'

'Is it?'

'Oh, if Siggy could see this—he'd love it!'

Daniel laughed. 'How you tempt me, Donna! Well, I

made a deal with the previous owners, there was no point in their taking things, really, when everything's fitted in, plumbed in and God knows what. It is rather nice, I must say.'

Half an hour later they were drinking coffee, sitting in the breakfast room which led off the kitchen. This was fitted with pine bench seats which had been especially made and the room overlooked the orchard. Donna was imagining how lovely it would be to sit there in the spring, when the blossom was on all the fruit trees. 'It's a beautiful house, Daniel, really beautiful! But why is it in such a state when you've been here for several weeks?'

He shrugged. 'Firstly I've been concentrating on getting everything in order at the office, secondly, I told you, I need help. I've got dozens of swatches, folders, samples of wallpaper, paint, panelling, carpeting, curtaining and so on—and I haven't had time to look at them yet. Nor have I had any thoughts on the kind of style, theme, I'm going to have.'

'But your furniture will suggest that to you!' Donna sighed impatiently. It was as though the past six weeks hadn't existed, they were talking as easily and as naturally as they used to, he was managing both to frustrate her and intrigue her all over again. 'Where *is* your furniture, Daniel? All the stuff from your last home?'

'My last home was my marital home.' He looked directly at her, making more than one point. 'When I sold it to come south, I put everything into storage. That settee in the living room belongs in my office, actually. But when I found this house, I decided I'd buy everything new, start from scratch. So I've auctioned every stick of furniture I used to own. Everything. It's called letting go of the past, Donna.'

That was their first awkward moment. She looked at him, nodding slightly but saying nothing. She didn't want to get on to the subject of pasts—his or hers. 'I—if you've got any eggs, I can rustle up an omelette.'

'Grief, woman, I want something to *eat*. I had breakfast hours ago. So come on, finish your coffee, do something about your hair and I'll take you out for lunch. It'll be the first in a series of rewards I'm going to give you.'

'For what?'

'For helping me to decorate and furnish this house, of course.' He was on his feet, clearing away their coffee cups.

'Daniel, I came here to discuss menus, not to——'

'Aw, Donna,' he said, without turning to look at her, 'don't keep your talents to yourself. You've got style, I've told you that. Share it with me, help me get this house sorted out.'

She got up, looking helplessly at the back of his head as he rinsed the coffee cups. She could think of nothing she would rather do than choose furniture and furnishings for this gorgeous house but, 'But, Daniel . . .'

'We'll start shopping tomorrow.'

'No, I—wait a minute! You said you were going out of town. You said you were going away for a couple of weeks.'

'Did I?' He turned, started walking towards her with a purposefulness that immediately alarmed her. He was unsmiling, looking at her in a way in which he had never looked at her before.

She was already backing away from him, already so alarmed and excited that she could hardly breathe.

'I lied,' he said simply, closing the distance between them rapidly yet without haste. 'I lied because I'd waited so long for your 'phone call, I wasn't prepared to wait another day to see you. I wanted you to come to me today, immediately.'

Donna's back was against the wall, her eyes moving rapidly from side to side, as if seeking a means of escape. Daniel stood in front of her, so close that she could catch the faint tang of his aftershave, the clean, masculine smell of him. 'Daniel, please, don't——'

A hand came out to catch hold of her chin, his hazel-green eyes locking on to hers with an intensity which made it impossible for her to break their contact. 'And here you are,' he finished. 'And you know what that tells me, don't you, Donna?'

'No! I'm here because——'

She got no further because Daniel was, finally, kissing her. He was kissing her with an intensity which drove all excuses and rationalisations out of her mind, drove all thoughts out of her mind. There was in that instant no room for thought, only emotion, only her response to that which she had wanted for so long. To be in his arms, to be held by him, to hold him in return. She responded hungrily, her lips parting willingly beneath the pressure of his as he kissed her long and hard.

CHAPTER ELEVEN

THE following few weeks were chaotic, at least for Donna. She amazed herself, wondering how she was managing to fit everything in. With Daniel she went from shop to shop in Richmond, looking at furniture, curtains, carpets. They went backwards and forwards to London, debating, deciding, taking infinite care that what they chose was right. They were both tireless, both thinking along the same lines, fortunately, as far as the house was concerned. Everything was going to be of the best, it was going to be deliciously luxurious, comfortable, modern, with nothing dark or drab in even the remotest corner.

It was exciting, watching it take shape. The decorators seemed to be in for ages, though in reality they weren't. Impatiently Donna waited to see the back of them, anxious to see what the carpets looked like when they were actually laid. After that, the curtains were delivered and furniture started arriving, some from stock, some which had been ordered specially.

All her free evenings were spent at Daniel's house. She was still catering for functions three, four or even five nights a week and was getting up at the crack of dawn in order to do her paper work. She was shattered but she was happy. Siggy had taken over the buying of food for the business, only too pleased to do what he could, only too pleased to see Donna on top of the world.

'Amazing what love can do for you,' he said to her on the Saturday before Daniel's official opening party.

They were having a well-earned, ten minute break and they were sitting in Donna's office, going through the diary for the following week. Daniel's party was on the Friday and, thankfully, they had nothing booked for the evening before. 'Thank God there's nothing booked for next Thursday,' Siggy went on. 'Because Friday's going to take it out of us all. We've never catered for two hundred before, Donna. It's a tall order. Are all the waitresses booked?'

She nodded. Actually, Siggy was looking forward to next Friday's function. He, Daniel and herself had had a long discussion about what would be served and Siggy had made so many suggestions that Daniel had ended up giving him carte blanche. 'I'll leave the entire thing to you, Siggy,' he'd said. 'You and Donna decide between you. I know I couldn't be in better hands.'

Siggy had been flattered by that. He, not Donna, had done all the planning and, with the instruction that no expense need be spared, Siggy was going overboard.

'Of course the waitresses are booked,' she said to him now. 'And for the record, I am not in love with Daniel.'

She spoke harshly, so harshly that Siggy sighed loudly. He could understand her denial to other people, but why deny it to him, why was she still denying it even to herself? 'I never mentioned Daniel's name,' he pointed out quietly. 'How do you know I wasn't talking about your love for your work? After all,' he added drily, 'that's something I can be certain about, isn't it? You're still driving yourself like a lunatic so I'll assume it really is work you're in love with—since you're still denying you're in love with anything or anyone else.'

Donna looked at him in exasperation. 'Siggy, can we get this straight once and for all? Daniel and I are just good friends.'

Siggy hooted, making no effort to hide his contempt of that remark. 'Well, that's your hang up, love.'

Changing the subject at once, Donna was appalled with herself for blushing furiously. What she had said to Siggy was true, but it was getting harder and harder to keep her relationship with Daniel on a purely platonic footing. Since the moment he'd kissed her she'd anticipated problems, had drawn the line very firmly ever since, on every occasion Daniel took her into his arms—which was every time she saw him. He had never pushed things, not once had he put any kind of pressure on her but the physical attraction was so strong between them that something would have to give, sometime.

She wanted Daniel. This was not the impression she gave him but it was something she absolutely could not deny to herself. Not this. She had gone home to her lonely bed on numerous occasions, aching for him, aroused even after her journey home, aroused by the mere memory of his kisses. Her desire for him was constant, even in his absence, and it frightened her.

That evening, five minutes before Daniel was due to collect her, Donna stood by her fireplace and looked hard and long at the photograph of her father. 'What would you think,' she asked aloud, 'if you knew what was happening between me and Daniel Conrad?'

Sighing, she put the photograph back in place. Near to it there was a bowl full of the roses Daniel kept her supplied with. They were in every room of her little house. Roses from Daniel. In season or out of season, he had always brought her roses. She glanced at her small carriage clock just as he rang the doorbell. She could set her watch by Daniel. If he said he would call for her at six-thirty, he meant six-thirty.

She smoothed down the skirt of the black velvet dress she was wearing. It was cocktail length, long-sleeved and cut low in the front. Daniel was taking her to the opera tonight, which would be a new experience for her, and she had chosen the dress with great care.

It was turned two in the morning when they got back. The November winds were driving a heavy downpour of rain so hard it was falling sideways, belting against the windows of his car. Neither of them noticed it, they were high from a fabulous evening. It had been for her an evening full of varying emotions. She had wept on seeing 'Madam Butterfly', she had felt undeniable pride during the interval, when she saw the admiring glances Daniel got from other women. Not that that was anything new, but he looked magnificent tonight in a formal dinner suit, his dark blond hair so thick and attractive, his beautiful, changeable eyes so full of interest in all that went on around him.

Later, over a superb meal, they had laughed, forgetting entirely the opera they had seen, at least for the time being. And then they had danced on the tiny dance-floor in the restuarant, content to hold one another without any conversation while they moved slowly to the soft, romantic music of a combo whose repertoire seemed endless.

'Are you falling asleep on me?' Daniel asked as they pulled up behind Donna's green Spitfire.

'Not a chance!' She giggled because she was in fact in danger of falling asleep. She was drowsy and content; the after effects of the wine she had drunk and the warmth of the car had almost lulled her into oblivion.

They made a dash for her front door, laughing like teenagers, shivering in the warmth of her tiny living room after the sudden shock of the cold wind.

'I'll put the coffee on,' Daniel told her. 'You turn that fire up as high as it'll go.'

Donna did just that, glad she had left the gas fire on half strength while they'd been out. The house didn't have central heating and it was going to be chilly when she went to bed. She made a mental note to buy some kind of heater for her bedroom. She slipped off her coat and curled up on the chair nearest the fire, wondering whether she were getting soft in her old age. Or was it just that she had spent so many evenings in the luxurious warmth of Daniel's house that her own place seemed cold by comparison?

She was sound asleep when he came back with the coffee. The next thing she knew, there was a warm hand against her cheek and a deep voice was asking her teasingly, 'I say, am I boring you?'

'Sorry . . .' She was smiling even before she opened her eyes. He was pulling her gently to her feet now and she was so tired, she could hardly stand up. She leaned heavily against him, resting her head on his shoulder. 'Daniel, would you mind if I skip coffee? I'm sorry but I'm just longing to go to bed.'

One arm came firmly around her waist, a hand came up to lift her chin and Daniel bent his head, claiming her mouth with an urgency which brought her immediately, fully awake. 'That makes two of us,' he murmured at length, his lips moving from her mouth to the side of her neck, along her throat. 'Let me stay with you tonight, Donna. I can't take much more of this.'

'Daniel!' She tried to step away from him but she was locked in the circle of his arms. He held her tightly against the length of his body, making her very well aware how much he wanted her. 'No! It's out of the question.'

'Out of the question?' he repeated, his brows drawing together over eyes which had darkened. 'Donna, you want me just as much as I want you.'

'No, no that's not true!' She said it firmly, panicking inwardly because he'd taken her by surprise. Until now he had accepted the situation when she'd drawn the line.

With an impatient groan he kissed her again and again, his hands keeping her hips locked firmly against him, his excitement communicating itself to her with such force that within minutes she was gasping, her breath coming shallow and fast as she fought to get even closer to him.

Daniel raised his head, his darkened eyes glittering triumphantly in the lamplight. 'Deny it now,' he challenged. 'Tell me about it, Donna. Tell me you don't want me to stay and make love to you.'

'I——' She couldn't look at him. 'Let me go, Daniel.'

Keeping one arm around her, he reached behind him, half turning her as they stood. He picked up the photograph from the mantlepiece and put it down again, face down, his voice curt as he spoke. 'Perhaps that makes you feel better? Can you say it now, now Daddy isn't looking?'

'Please, Daniel, I don't know what you mean! You're barking up the wrong tree, Let go of me, please.'

He didn't let go of her, he held her tightly, looking deep into her eyes. 'For God's sake, Donna, I'm in love with you! Don't you realise that?'

'*No!*' She wrenched away from him, covering her ears with her hands. 'I don't want to hear this, don't talk to me in those terms, please!'

'In *those terms*?' He was staring at her. 'What's the matter, have I said something vulgar?' He caught hold of her, shaking her. 'Donna, I'm in love with you and I want you. I can't go on much longer like this— competing with this obsession of yours. I want you to be my wife, I want you to share your life with me!'

Horrified, she jerked her arms from his grasp and sat, trembling from head to foot. She couldn't even look at him. 'Please go,' she whispered. 'I'll never marry you, don't ever ask me again. Don't talk to me of love!'

'Why?' he demanded. 'Because I am who I am, is that it? Is that it, Donna?'

She closed her eyes. 'I . . . no. Because I'm not in love with you. It's as simple as that.'

She heard clearly his parting shot as he let himself out. 'You're lying. But don't worry, I'm a patient man, I'll play your game a little bit longer.'

In the sudden silence of the room she opened her eyes and stared at the place where he had been a moment ago. His last sentence had made no sense to her, none at all. She wasn't playing a game. She didn't love him. Nor did she want him to love her. Not her. Not him. It couldn't be. Between the two of them, it just couldn't be.

CHAPTER TWELVE

'DONNA? Are you all right?'

The offices were buzzing with conversation. People stood around in groups, eating, talking in earnest. She hadn't expected Daniel's official opening party to be a jolly affair, it was purely to impress his customers and he and his staff had spent the past two hours concentrating on them, talking to them and answering questions, showing them around the premises.

Donna and her staff had moved among those present quietly and efficiently, keeping everyone happy as far as food and drinks were concerned. The party was proving a success, achieving, as far as she could tell, what it was supposed to achieve, yet she felt curiously detached from it all. She felt, in fact, decidedly unwell.

'You look like death,' Siggy went on, speaking quietly so nobody else could hear.

'I'm not feeling too good,' she admitted. 'But come on, it's time to start clearing up.'

'Go and sit in Daniel's office. The girls and I can cope.'

'No.' Donna shook her head stubbornly. 'I'm just tired, that's all. It'll pass.'

An argument ensued, a quiet one which Siggy lost. He went out of the room, leaving Donna to do what she wanted, and went in search of Daniel. Daniel would sort her out.

'Donna! What the hell are you doing? Get back indoors at once!' Daniel was heading towards her, Siggy hard on his heels, as she was opening the doors of the Transit van, parked in the yard at the rear of the main building.

'We have to start loading things,' she protested, her hand going involuntarily to her throbbing temple. The

129

wind was whipping her hair around her face and she blamed this for the sudden distortion of the lights from the office block. For split seconds she couldn't remember where she was and she looked through the darkness at the rapidly advancing figures of Siggy and Daniel with only vague recognition. 'I'm ... Daniel, I'm ...'

She passed out at the precise moment he reached for her, gathering her into his arms just as her legs gave way.

She came to in his private office, lying on the settee and knowing an overwhelming panic as she registered how dim the room was. Some light was coming through the reeded windows which separated them from the corridor, and the hum of voices seemed deafeningly loud in her ears.

'Donna? Donna!' A hand tightened around hers, Daniel's voice sounding both annoyed and fearful as he repeated her name.

Her eyes closed and opened again and this time everything fell into perspective. The voices had receded and she realised that only the desk lamp was on in Daniel's office. 'I'm—all right now. Just ... tired.' Her eyes closed again.

'You're just stupid! No, don't try to get up. Keep your head down, give yourself a chance.' He sighed, relieved, his fingers raking through his hair as he knelt by her side. 'For heaven's sake, Donna, what am I going to do about you? Why didn't you tell me how bad you were feeling? I said keep *still*. If Siggy hadn't come looking for me, you'd be lying outside in the rain now, catching your death!'

'Don't exaggerate,' she groaned. 'I'm okay.'

'Like hell! I'm taking you home, now. Stay put till I come back with your coat.'

Donna's eyes flew open. 'You can't leave your party! Your customers——'

'To hell with my customers,' he said angrily. 'My staff can deal with them. You're more important than my customers, Donna, and one of these days you might start to feel the same way about me—as far as your customers are concerned.'

The office door closed and Donna lay perfectly still because she had little choice. Her limbs felt as though they were coated with six inches of lead. She moaned inwardly at the awful sensation of it, at the point Daniel had just made with such a bite in his voice.

Christmas, that's what that had been all about. He had asked her to go away with him to his house in Sardinia at Christmas, and she had refused. Quite apart from the fact that she didn't want to be alone with him under the same roof for even one night, how could she possibly get away? At Christmas, the busiest time of the year? It was impossible and she'd told him so, last night when this conversation had taken place. Her Christmas bookings had been made long ago.

'Then come to Lincoln with me,' he'd gone on. 'You *have* got Christmas day off and the two days after it. Come with me and we'll spend Christmas with my parents. Besides, I'd like you to meet my sister and her family, they don't live far from Dad.'

'No,' she'd said quickly, irritating him. But really, what else could she have said? The very idea of staying with Richard Conrad and his wife—the idea of *merry making* in the house of Richard Conrad was more than she could envisage.

'That's what I thought you'd say.' Daniel had sighed heartily. 'Well, I'm going. To Lincoln, I mean. I'll go before Christmas since I'm not going to be able to see you for umpteen days leading up to it.'

So that's how it had been left. She wouldn't see Daniel for about three weeks, in total. But she had told herself it was just as well, that a break from one another was just what they needed. What she needed. Maybe then she would be able to decide quite how she felt about him.

'Donna? Feeling any better now?' She breathed a sigh of relief when he came back into his office with her coat. The edge had gone from his voice and in the soft light of the desk lamp, his eyes were gentle on her now. 'You know,' he said, smiling down at her, 'you're the most beautiful idiot it's ever been my privilege to know.'

Things continued like that, off and on, for the next couple of weeks. It turned out that Donna had a severe dose of 'flu and for days she shivered and sneezed, thinking at first that it was just a cold. But she stayed in bed for a solid week. Even if the doctor had allowed her to get up, Daniel would not. He was as firm as she knew only too well he could be. In other words, he was immovable.

Daniel stopped everything, dropped everything, he brought a suitcase of clothes from his house, made up the bed-settee in her dining room and moved in with her to look after her.

It was a curious time. As if he couldn't stop himself, there were moments when he attacked her again and again about what he called her obsession with work. Donna took it without argument; she simply hadn't the strength to argue with him. There again there were moments when he showed such tenderness that she wanted to cry, times when he held her hand, wiped the perspiration from her forehead and murmured words of encouragement. 'You'll feel better soon, darling. It's hit you so hard because you were run down to begin with. Rest, that's all you really need.'

But that wasn't quite true. She needed Daniel, too, more and more she was realising how important he was to her, though she didn't want to make a life with him. She couldn't even consider the idea of marrying him. He had said nothing more about that, much to her relief. He hadn't even broached the subject.

There was also laughter during her illness. Daniel was not, to put it mildly, the world's best cook, and the first two omelettes he made for her bore a striking resemblance to scrambled eggs.

Siggy took over when he could. He was handling

everything very well as far as the business was concerned, much to his own surprise, and when he was free he came round to Donna's and cooked for her, himself and Daniel.

She was allowed up at the start of the second week but she couldn't do much. Still weak in the legs, she was very easily tired even by walking from one room to the next. On her fourth day up she felt tons better and she made breakfast to prove it.

'Where do you think you're going?' Daniel asked, peering over his newspaper when she made a move to get up.

'To wash up.'

'Sit down and behave yourself, cooking breakfast was quite enough. I'll wash up. Primitive notion that it is,' he added, looking heavenward. 'If that kitchen of yours were big enough to swing a cat in, you could have a dishwasher installed.'

'Where are you going now?' he asked her about an hour later, when they were sitting by the fire in the living room. He had been talking to his works manager for quite a while on the 'phone, while Donna had been dozing almost against her will. She felt very frustrated, lacking energy like this. She was tired again.

'I'm going upstairs for my emery boards, my nails are in a shocking state.'

'I'll get them,' he said cheerfully. 'I have to go to the bathroom in any case. Where are they?'

'In my desk drawer, I think.'

'Where else?' Daniel grinned at her. 'Any other woman would keep them in her dressing table.'

She laughed as he left her but when he came back, what remained of the smile on her face was immediately dispelled.

In his hand there was a piece of paper and in his eyes there was a look which was very far removed from teasing. He was angry, very. 'What the hell is this?' he demanded, thrusting the paper at her.

Donna glanced at it, recognising it at once. It was

another letter from the agents who handled her house in Lincolnshire and she hadn't answered it. It had arrived some three weeks earlier and she had shoved it in her desk drawer, intending to answer it when she'd reached a decision about its contents. 'It's—it's an offer for the purchase of my house in the Wolds.'

'I can see that!'

'I'm not sure what to do about it. I—it's from my agents.' She looked up at him, unsure why he was so angry.

'I can see that,' he said again. 'I can see also that it's not the first offer you've had! They're referring to the figure you refused weeks ago and they're making you a new offer, saying that your tenant very much wants to buy the house and so they've upped the price. A price which is some thousands of pounds more than your own agents think it's worth.

'Donna, what the hell are you thinking about? Why haven't you accepted? They're even prepared to do a deal over the furniture!' He whipped the paper from her hands, staring at it then staring at her. 'Grief, woman, you've got a ready buyer for the place, lock, stock and barrel at an extremely good price. What *have* you told them? Have you 'phoned them? *What* is happening here?'

'I haven't given them any answer,' she retorted wearily. 'I—just can't decide whether to sell the place or not. I'm not sure yet.'

'Not sure about what?' He sat, seemingly at a loss to understand her.

'I'm not sure about anything, Daniel. Not sure whether I can let go of my home——'

'*Home?* That place isn't home to you! You don't belong there!'

'Daniel, please! Leave me alone. I'm simply not sure yet whether I want to take the money and use it to expand my business. Don't say anything else, please. I don't want to get on to this subject and I'm not up to an argument. I'm just not sure what I want to do with my life from now on, that's all.'

Daniel began to say something and checked himself. He looked strained, as she did, the lines of his face very tense suddenly. Without looking at her again, he got to his feet.

'Where are you going?' she asked, her eyes widening in despair.

Daniel walked through to the place which was his temporary bedroom, picked up his jacket then sat heavily in a chair. He closed his eyes, acknowledging wearily that this was not the right moment to propose to her again. Nor was it the right moment to tell her that which she had to be told—sooner or later. She still looked as white as a sheet, not at all well. He got up, went back to the living room.

'Donna,' he said softly, taking hold of her hand as she looked up at him with eyes so big and blue they never failed to move him. 'You know, at this moment I don't know which I want to do most—make love to you or give you a spanking. You are driving me slowly round the bend. For the moment, I'll do neither. I have to go into my office for a couple of hours. There's a problem which needs sorting out.'

She nodded as he let go of her hand, her smile small and half-hearted, uncertain, reflecting the confusion in her mind. 'Daniel,' she whispered. 'I—want to thank you. For everything, for all that you've done for me these past couple of weeks, for the way you've looked after me.'

He bent to kiss her, her arms went eagerly around his neck and she clung to him, enjoying the sheer strength of him. She had no idea what she would have done without him while she'd been ill. It had been good to have someone to lean on, someone to look after her.

Daniel detached himself and moved to the porch, one hand on the handle of the door. 'I love you,' he said simply. 'I think that explains everything. When are you going to be able to say the same thing to me, Donna? When are you going to admit to yourself that you love me?'

He closed the door before she could utter a sound, leaving her to stare after him with eyes which had filled with tears. She didn't love him. She wished she could, but she did not. Not for a moment did she doubt he loved her, however, not any more, even though she couldn't understand why he did. He had shown her how much he loved her while he had been here, looking after her. He had neglected everything else in his life, everything but her.

But she didn't want Daniel's love any more than she wanted to love him. When he came back from the office, she told him firmly it was time he went back to his house now, back to his own home.

He laughed humourlessly. 'Scares the living daylights out of you, doesn't it?'

'I don't know what you mean.'

'Yes you do. Being loved by me. Being wanted by me. The prospect of our being under the same roof now that you're feeling better. But don't panic . . .' He held up a hand, a hint of amusement creeping into his eyes. 'I'll leave after dinner tonight.'

He did, too, very shortly after dinner. 'I'll ring you late tomorrow morning, Donna. If you're feeling up to it, I'll take you out to lunch.'

'Up to it? Daniel, I'm going to *work* tomorrow.'

'No, you're *not*. *No way!* You're by no means up to that.' He put his suitcase down, wagging a finger at her as if she were a naughty child.

She sighed inwardly. Let him find out for himself where she would be tomorrow. There was no point in arguing with this man, he was as stubborn as a mule. 'All right, Daniel, all right,' she said non-committally, not exactly lying to him. But she was going into work, she simply had to. It was December and it was all happening—parties of every description. She was needed; it wouldn't be fair to Siggy for her to take any more time off.

By mid morning the next day, Donna was thinking about the old saying—a stitch in time. She felt wretched, totally without stamina, was regretting her decision yet knowing she had really had no choice. Siggy played hell with her for coming in, so did Una, and at ten minutes to twelve Daniel turned up.

Donna had just sat down for a cup of coffee in her office, her head was in her hands as Daniel walked in and she straightened up at once, making a determined effort to appear normal.

'Daniel? What is it?' He was saying nothing, just standing in the doorway, looking at her. There was an odd expression on his face and it frightened her. It was something beyond anger, it was fury.

'So here you are,' he said at length. 'Well, I've come to ask one question of you, Donna, just one question.'

She swallowed, her mouth suddenly feeling bone dry.

'Will you come away with me this weekend? No strings,' he added quickly. 'I just want you to get some rest, that's all. We'll go to a nice quiet hotel I know of in the country.'

Relief flooded over her. Was that all? 'It sounds good, Daniel,' she said honestly. She flipped open the diary on her desk, appealing to him to understand. 'But I just can't. Look. Look at Saturday's bookings. Going away this weekend is out of the question.' And the following weekend would be Christmas. Daniel would be gone by then, she was well aware of that and she wasn't relishing the idea.

Daniel looked, not at the diary but at her. He looked hard and long, then he nodded, his voice almost inaudible. 'Then I'll see you in January.'

'In ... *January?* ... But—but——'

'I'm leaving for Lincoln today and I'm staying there till the New Year. There's no point in my staying in Surrey when I don't need to, when there's no incentive. Goodbye, Donna.'

She murmured the word in response but Daniel had already gone. Without a kiss, without so much as another word. She put her arms on her desk, put her head on them and started crying softly. It wasn't fair of him to do this. It wasn't fair of him to expect her to go away with him this weekend.

Well, let him go to Lincoln, let him go to hell! If she could not cope without him for a few weeks, there was something drastically wrong with her.

CHAPTER THIRTEEN

DONNA threw herself into her work as best she could. The trouble was that in no way was she functioning as she used to. It wasn't Daniel's absence, it wasn't the fact that he didn't ring her, it was that she felt ill. Constantly, she felt as if she still had 'flu. She did her utmost to hide this from other people and she managed to keep going but at times she felt so exhausted she could hardly see straight.

Chaos reigned throughout Christmas Eve. The pâtisserie was jammed full of customers from opening time till closing time while in the back of the premises, Donna, Siggy and Una worked like slaves. A light snow was falling but they had the back doors open regardless, it was impossibly hot in the kitchen, what with all three of them working flat out.

They had a double booking for that night, it was something Donna had committed herself to months earlier and was now regretting. All she wanted to do was to lie down and sleep for a week. For two weeks. She felt sure she could, she smiled at the very idea of such luxury. But she wouldn't want to sleep for more than two weeks because by then Daniel would be back.

Daniel. He was constantly on her mind no matter what she was doing. Fortunately she had no time to feel blue, no time actually to miss him because even if he'd stayed in Surrey she couldn't have spent time with him.

Tomorrow would be different, of course. Tomorrow was Christmas Day and then—then how would she feel? Being alone? Still, there was January to look forward to, January bringing Daniel's return. It was the one month of the year she normally hated, its bleakness, freezing cold, lack of bookings. She had not a solitary booking for the coming January—after the first, that was. It was traditionally a quiet month.

By the time she and her staff were loading up the vans that evening, the snow had stopped and the weather seemed to be turning colder by the minute. Donna was paying her waitresses triple time for working Christmas Eve. She'd had to, otherwise she'd have had no volunteers.

She and Siggy went separate ways, Donna in the Mini and Siggy in the big van. He was to drop the waitresses and some of the food at a house in Kingston Vale and then double back to join her for the one hundred strong party in Teddington, at the home of a partner of Kieren's. Kieren wouldn't be there, though, he had flown up to Scotland to spend Christmas with his sister. He, his parents and his latest girlfriend.

It was almost one in the morning when Donna got away from Teddington. Siggy had left earlier, having to go back to pick up staff and belongings from the other house, so Donna was alone in the Mini and feeling as though her eyes were full of grit. She could hardly keep them open.

That was how the accident happened. Donna knew nothing at all about it, not a thing. She did not remember hitting the lamp-post, she didn't remember the sound of breaking glass or the blow to her head against the side of the van as the vehicle crunched violently into concrete.

Her first memory, her first awareness was of a blinding light as she tried to open her eyes. Then there was the pain in her head, as though someone were kicking it with a metal-capped boot. After that there was blackness, for how long, she had no way of knowing. Consciousness came and went and with it the white light and the pain. At one point she thought she could make out the outlines of people bending over her, talking softly to themselves. At another point there was her awareness of an alien smell and then she was being moved—wheeled on some sort of trolley.

She opened her eyes once to stare long enough at a peculiar shape to her left. It was minutes before she recognised it as a water jug, before she realised she was in a hospital bed with curtains drawn around it. There was nobody else present then. When next she opened her eyes, she was somewhere else, not in a bed with curtains around it but in a room with white walls, a small room which contained another smell—a familiar fragrance.

Roses.

She opened her eyes. There was a water jug in this place, too, and beside it there was a vase which contained roses, red roses. 'Daniel?'

'Take it easy, Miss Kent. You're all right.' She felt a hand on her shoulder, a male voice telling her exactly where she was, that she was concussed and would be as right as rain in a few days. She also had three cracked ribs.

'Daniel?'

'He's outside,' the voice said. 'With Mr Gee. You can see your friends tomorrow, I can't allow you any visitors yet. Can you open your eyes again? Tell me how you're feeling?'

There wasn't much to tell. She hurt. Everywhere. The doctor explained to her that she had skidded in the Mini. There was, he said, black ice on the roads and she had skidded and hit a lamp-post.

'I—can't remember anything, anything at all about it.'

'Retrograde amnesia,' came the calm reply. 'Don't bother trying to remember, the concussion is responsible for your being unable to and it really doesn't matter, does it? You're very lucky to have got off so lightly, lucky nobody else was involved.' Then the doctor was gone. She slept.

There was a nurse in the room when next she opened her eyes, asking at once for a glass of water. 'What time is it?'

'Ten in the evening.'

'The evening? But—what day is this?'

'It's Christmas Day.' The nurse, who was probably in her thirties and was attractive, poured a glass of water and gave Donna an encouraging smile.

'Then—Daniel isn't here,' she said dully. She made an effort to sit up and regretted it instantly, yelping with pain in the area of her ribs.

'Happy Christmas!' the nurse said cheerfully. 'Come on, let me help. Take it slowly now . . . Daniel's your boyfriend, is he? The tall man with broad shoulders, dark blond hair?'

Donna nodded, which was something else she regretted. Everything seemed to be throbbing, her head, her entire body. She knew for certain that Daniel had been in the hospital; the roses had to be from him, only he could find roses on Christmas day. In season or out of season he gave her roses, always roses.

'Oh, he's here, all right,' the nurse went on, her voice sounding resigned. 'He's been pacing the corridors for hours. Another gentleman was with him when I came on duty, a Mr Gee, but he had the good sense to take our advice and go home, spend his Christmas doing something more conventional. But your Mr Conrad,' she added grimly, 'is immovable. He said he's staying till he can see for himself that you're all right and he doesn't care how long that takes. It was he who gave us instructions to put you in a private room, in case you're wondering. Now then, would you like to see him for a few minutes?'

Donna hadn't been wondering about the room, she was wondering about the accident and how it happened. Had she really skidded on black ice? Or had she . . . 'Nurse, I—I can't remember what happened to me. I'm—I have a feeling I fell asleep at the wheel.'

The nurse blinked. 'You hadn't been drinking.'

'No, no. I'd been . . . working.' She closed her eyes. Daniel was going to be cross with her, she just knew it. He'd been cross when she caught influenza, so . . . She looked at the flowers again. The nurse was asking her whether she felt up to a visit, stressing it would be only for a few minutes, on doctor's orders. 'It's just that he looks pretty rough himself,' she went on. 'And he insists on staying till he sees you. Sister Atkinson told me he's been here since the middle of last night—said something about his driving down from Lincoln after getting a call from Mr Gee.'

'Send him in,' Donna said firmly. Cross or not, she was longing to see him, she was very much in need of Daniel's quiet strength right now.

But that wasn't what she got. And she had been wrong in thinking he would be cross. Daniel Conrad was beside himself, so angry with her that to begin with he could barely form a sentence.

After the nurse departed, Donna waited for several minutes. She had begun to think he had gone home when suddenly the door of her room was flung open and in he came, unshaven, white-faced and looking as though he'd aged ten years since she'd last seen him.

'Donna! What the—how did—I've been half out of my *mind*!' He slammed her door closed with total disregard for his surroundings, not to mention the way she was feeling, and advanced on her with a fury unlike anything she'd ever seen in him before.

'Daniel, I——' That was as far as she got. She shrank visibly in the bed, staring at him as he roared at her.

'What are you?' he demanded. 'Absolutely crazy? On a mission of self-destruction? You do realise you could so easily have killed yourself last night? Of course you do! You think you fell asleep at the wheel? That's what you just told the nurse, isn't it? God in heaven, it's all I've been thinking about all day. I don't doubt it for a second! You were ill to begin with and I don't doubt for one second that you've been working every day since I last saw you. You won't listen to anyone, will you, Donna? You follow——'

'Daniel, Daniel, please!' She couldn't stand this, not now. Her hand went up to her throbbing head and tears poured down her face.

But it was as if Daniel couldn't even see her, let alone hear her protests. He talked right over them. 'You follow your own inner voice—which is all well and good except that in your case it's going to destroy you. You are programmed for self-destruction, doing exactly what your father did! Except that his death was an accidental one. But you don't believe that, do you, madam? Well, I happen to know that it was, I happen to know that he was on his way to meet his *mistress* when he died!'

'*What?*' Donna's voice pierced the air, cutting straight through his ranting.

'*Mister Conrad!*' The nurse was back, standing in the doorway and glaring at him. 'Please leave! How dare you——'

Daniel hadn't even noticed the woman. He was staring at Donna, his eyes bright and greener than they'd ever appeared. 'You heard me. I said your precious, marvellous, beloved Daddy was on his way to a rendezvous with his mistress when he smashed himself to smithereens!'

'I don't believe you!' Donna's voice was full and loud, the shock of what he was saying to her bringing forth a reserve of strength from somewhere. 'I don't believe that for one minute. Now get out. Get *out*!'

That was what the nurse was ordering, too. 'Mister Conrad, will you please leave this room at once. *At once!*' She marched up to Daniel and took hold of him by the arm as if willing to eject him bodily. Perhaps she was willing but she was not able.

Daniel pulled his arm from her grasp, his eyes not leaving Donna's for an instant. 'I've never lied to you yet,' he said in a slightly lower voice. 'You believe it. You'd better. I've got my facts right, Donna. *Your father was in love with my stepmother and on the day he died he was on his way to meet her.* I had this straight from Delia herself. She was on the verge of divorcing my father and you can take her word for it, if not mine, that suicide was the last thing on your father's mind!'

Suddenly there was stillness, total silence. Nobody moved or spoke. Both the nurse and Donna were staring at Daniel as though they'd never seen a man before. He closed his eyes, his hand going up to cover them as his head bowed and he swore so viciously at himself that both women would have been shocked if they were capable of being shocked further.

The nurse spoke first. 'Mr Conrad,' she said quietly, 'I think that's more than enough, don't you?'

Daniel looked at her for the first time, his head moving slowly up and down. With pure agony in his eyes, he looked at Donna for several seconds before turning to walk quietly out of the room.

The room was shifting before Donna's eyes, she concentrated all her efforts on speaking to the retreating figure as though her life depended on it. 'Don't ever come back, Daniel. I never want to see you again as long as I live!' Then, as hysteria rose in her throat like a tangible lump, she screamed so shrilly that the entire room seemed to reverberate. 'Liar! Liar, liar, *liar!*'

CHAPTER FOURTEEN

'CAN I tell him that?' Siggy asked anxiously. 'Can I ring him and tell him?'

Donna nodded. It no longer hurt to do so. It was New Year's Eve. She had been kept in the hospital mainly for observation because of the concussion and was to be discharged the next day. Apart from the still painful ribs, a discomfort she would have to live with for some time, she was feeling perfectly well except for the tiredness. During her week in bed she had done nothing but think, sleep and eat, yet she still felt exhausted.

She was also utterly calm. She had sobbed over the information Daniel had given her, but not for long. She had wondered about it, too, but again, not for long. Days ago she had known without a doubt that he had told her the truth. It had left her ... accepting ... understanding some things to a certain extent and feeling so calm inside that she wondered whether her personality had been irreversibly altered.

'Yes, Siggy.' She reached for him as he bent to kiss her goodbye, resting her hand against his face in the hope that that would convey more adequately than words her appreciation of his friendship. 'You can tell Daniel I'll see him tonight.'

It was this more than anything that brought his old smile back to his face. 'Thank God for that! He's driven me up the wall this past week, calling in every day and 'phoning, asking how you were, what you'd said, whether you'd see him.'

'I know,' she said softly, 'I know.' She could well imagine the hell Daniel had been through this past week, having been forbidden to see her. He had been to the hospital several times, at different hours, during the first couple of days and had received the same message over and over: Miss Kent will not see you.

Well, Miss Kent would see him tonight. At visiting time. Just this once before she was discharged. After that . . . she didn't know. She was going to go away for a while. There were things she had to do.

'Don't forget your Specials.' Siggy stabbed a finger in the direction of a silver cake box as he walked away. 'You could still use a little more weight.'

She smiled and waved as he left the room, her eyes going to the box of cakes which were named and sold as 'Siggy's Specials'—choux pastry buns filled with fresh cream and topped with a lattice-work of two differently coloured and flavoured icings. Embossed on the box in a heavier, darker shade of silver were the words 'Kent Catering Services'. She closed her eyes. Maybe one day those words would revert to what they once had read: 'Gee's Pâtisserie'.

And maybe not.

She would have to take one step at a time.

The door to Donna's room opened softly at seven-thirty on the dot that evening. She watched Daniel hovering there, seeing for the first time ever that he was capable of moments of uncertainty. Something constricted in her chest, her heart started to hammer rapidly, yet her mind was standing guard over her emotions and her smile of welcome was a cool one.

'Come in, Daniel.'

He approached the bed almost tentatively, his arms full of roses, fresh, tight little buds which couldn't fail to delight her. She had never told him they were her favourite flowers. Despite his absence she had received roses daily, via Siggy. 'From Daniel,' he had said on every visit. 'With his love.'

She thanked Daniel for them now and he put them down wordlessly on her bedside cabinet. Where once they would have joked about the profusion of flowers already in the room, let alone those she had given to other patients, nothing was said for the moment.

'I—that wasn't the way I intended to tell you about your father, Donna.' He stood, his eyes searching hers frantically. He was not happy with what he saw ... but it could, he knew, have been worse. Much worse. At least she was smiling a little.

'I know,' she said softly. 'Perhaps that was the only way you could tell me, in a fit of fury. Sit down, Daniel.'

'I wanted to tell you a hundred times before. I—tried to tell you almost seven years ago, when you were eighteen, that day I came to your house.'

Wordlessly, Donna accepted this. On hearing it she knew that that too was the truth. She had done a great deal of thinking, of memory-searching, in the past seven days. 'Please sit down, Daniel.'

He sat, drawing a chair close to the bed but not too close. He didn't reach for her hand. The room was too still, she was too quiet. He was scared of whatever was coming. She wasn't even looking at him now.

'This is what all the gossip was about, isn't it?' she asked at length. 'The affair between my father and your stepmother?'

'Partly.'

'How come I didn't hear it? I've been thinking back, I think even Daddy's accountant had an inkling.'

'He might have,' came the honest and quiet reply. 'But he probably didn't know who the woman was. Very few people knew that. The gossip was about all sorts of things, I suppose, your father's bankruptcy, his accident, the fact that he was seeing *someone*. It isn't surprising you knew nothing about this, Donna. You were away at college when the gossip was rife, and both Joseph and Delia were extremely discreet. They covered their tracks impeccably and when they ... saw each other ... it was always somewhere miles from town. Your father couldn't tell you for obvious reasons, plus the fact that you were so young and probably wouldn't understand.'

She looked at him then. 'Do you understand it?'

'Yes.' He held her gaze unwaveringly. 'Yes, darling. And so would you, if you talked to Delia about it. I—she's willing to do that, if you'd like to talk to her. All she asks is that you and she meet privately, without my father being there. Which is fair enough,' he added, 'because there's no point in upsetting Dad again. As far as he's concerned, it's all in the past.'

'You mean he knew? Your father knew about the affair?'

'All my family knew. I—it's a fairly long story and I really think you'd be better talking to Delia than to me about it.' Daniel took a small card from his pocket and put it on the cabinet. 'That's my parents' address and 'phone number. Delia's usually at home. Dad still works but not full-time, not every day, so if you ring her, please be careful, be discreet.'

'I don't want to talk to her,' Donna said hastily. 'You—you've obviously told her about us?'

'I told her weeks ago, one weekend when I went to Lincoln, during that time you and I weren't seeing each other. I told her then, in private, that I was in love with you and wanted to marry you. I told her also how strong your resentment of me was, I told her everything, Donna. Everything. She urged me to tell you the truth, about her and your father. I said I'd tried to do just that a hundred times but I could never seem to find the right moment.'

He sighed, looking at her apologetically. 'I ... was afraid to tell you, Donna. I ... simply didn't know what effect it would have on you.' He looked at her quickly, wishing he could gauge what effect it had had on her, wishing he could know what was in her mind now. Her expression told him nothing; she looked very withdrawn, she was still avoiding his eyes. 'Donna, please try to understand my point of view. You see, when you were eighteen my only thought was to tell you so you'd stop thinking your father committed suicide. I realised what a devastating effect that can have on a person, epecially one so young. But you wouldn't let me talk to you, no way would you do that. In any case it would have been very difficult because Joseph was obviously some kind of hero to you.

'Recently, when I discovered you were still thinking along the same lines, after all those years, I was horrified. I knew I had no choice but to tell you, yet you still appeared to idolise your father as much as ever, which made it difficult.' Daniel spread his hands in a gesture of helplessness. 'And, God help me, I was scared to tell you because I'd fallen in love with you and just didn't know how you'd react. I don't know how that happened, it just did. It hit me like a tidal wave and believe me, nobody was more surprised than I.'

Donna said nothing to that. 'What did Delia say?' she asked quietly, her mind struggling to reconcile a hundred thoughts and emotions, all of which were at variance.

Disappointed by her lack of response to his statement, Daniel closed his eyes briefly, keeping only to the facts as he went on. 'She sympathised with me, with my predicament. It was difficult for her, too. I mean, that of all the women in the world, it is you I want. She said I had to tell you the facts straight away, that I'd never get anywhere with you till I put an end to your resentment of me. She said also that I should tell my father about you, which I did.'

Donna's eyes shot straight to his. 'And what did he say?'

'He said it's a small world.' Daniel shrugged wearily, running a hand through his hair. He looked ghastly, as tired as she felt, and Donna sympathised with him inwardly but she simply couldn't bring herself to show it, to reach for his hand, to make any kind of gesture.

'Dad was great about it, actually. He said he'd always liked you, not that he knew you all that well. It was a difficult scene for all of us, Donna, you can imagine. Delia was ill at ease throughout the discussion which followed. Still . . .' He got to his feet, his hands shoved deep into his pockets, and moved restlessly around the room. 'The upshot was that Dad agreed entirely with Delia, said you had to be told everything as soon as possible. I—they suggested then that we all spent Christmas together. They—I—we'd hoped it would be out in the open and everything would be all right by then.' He laughed humourlessly, his eyes beseeching as he paused by the foot of her bed. 'Donna, for God's sake will you say something? Tell me what you're thinking!'

She shook her head in confusion. 'I'm trying to take it all in. You'll have to give me time, Daniel. Can't you guess what I'm thinking now?' Her voice rose slightly with a note of panic which was plain to hear. 'I'm thinking your father forced my father into bankruptcy as an act of *revenge* because Daddy was about to steal his wife!'

'No!' he said firmly, almost shouting now. He took hold of the rail of the bed, gripping it tightly as he would like to take hold of Donna, to shake some sense into her. 'You see? This is another reason why I put off telling you. I *knew* you'd think that, but it isn't so. Donna, if you have any feeling at all for me, you've got to believe I'm telling the truth. It was *after* the creditors' meeting, *after* the decision had been taken that Dad learned of the affair. Delia was going to leave him for your father, bankrupt or not. She loved him, Donna. Please, *please* talk to her about it.'

'If I decide to, why the need for discretion?' she shot at him. 'If everything you're saying is true, if you and your parents discussed the matter openly, why should Delia and I meet in secret?'

'I didn't say you should meet in secret, I said it would be better to meet in private. Discussing it was very difficult for all of us. Both Delia and my father did that for my sake. Neither of them wanted to bring up the past but they both agreed you should be told everything.'

Daniel turned away, unable to bear the look on her

face. She doubted him, that much was clear. God, this was difficult! And there was something else she had yet to be told . . . 'Darling, it would be impossible for Delia to talk to you about Joseph if my father were present. That ought to be obvious to you. And I beg of you, talk to her, listen to her version. It's not as sordid as it sounds. She and your father loved one another. You see, there's something else you have to know . . . they—their affair had been going on for some years.'

'*What?* What do you mean, for some years?' She was staring at him, feeling as though the entire structure of her thinking was coming apart. Surely this didn't mean that her father had been carrying on with Delia Conrad while his wife was alive? Not while . . . surely not while Donna's mother was alive! 'Daniel, *answer me!*'

'Donna——' He came swiftly to her side, reaching for her hand.

'Don't *touch* me! Just *tell* me!'

Daniel sank into a chair, his fingers rubbing cruelly over closed eyes as he shook his head. 'Christ, this is so unfair, so bloody unfair! The sins of the parents—yes, for years, Donna. Oh, I don't know how long exactly, but certainly they were seeing each other while your mother was alive. This is yet another reason why I found it so hard to tell you,' he added dully.

Silence reigned.

In the silence, in the stillness, they both felt a million miles from one another. In those awful minutes Donna wanted desperately to reach for him, to be held tightly by him. Yet she couldn't even look at him. It wasn't her father's unfaithfulness of itself that was upsetting her so, it was the shattering of the illusions she had lived under for so many years. So her parents' marriage had not been the blissful relationship she had always thought it was! Neither had Richard Conrad's to Delia, for that matter.

Had her mother known? she wondered. She hoped not, she desperately hoped not. It was a question she'd have given a great deal to know the answer to. Her poor mother, she'd been so unwell for so long, and all that time ...

In that instant, Donna felt such a hatred for her father, it almost choked her. Her hatred for Delia Conrad was even greater.

She looked at Daniel, realising that it was impossible to go on with him in any way, shape or form. The sins of the parents ... yes, it was unfair. But there was a barrier between her and Daniel now far stronger than there had ever been before.

'Daniel, please go now.'

He paled visibly, his face turning quite grey. 'Donna, I beg of you, talk to Delia. Listen to her version, you must, you owe it to your father, if not to her.'

'I don't owe anybody anything,' she said coldly, 'including you.' She reached for the water jug, lifting a hand to stop him as Daniel tried to assist.

'What are you going to do?' he asked quietly. 'I feel I'm entitled to know.'

She shrugged. 'I had plans but ... now I don't know. I still have a set of keys to your villa in Sardinia, I was going to ask you if I might go there for a rest.'

'Alone?'

'Of course, alone,' she snapped. 'What do you think?'

Daniel picked up the card he'd put on the cabinet, he took out a pen and started writing on the back of it. 'I don't think anything,' he said without looking at her. He didn't want to look at her, didn't want to see again the cold anger in her eyes. For some time to come, whatever she wanted to do he would have to comply. He realised that.

He put the card back. 'I've written the address for you. It's just fifteen minutes' drive from Cagliari airport. There are three airfields on the island, make sure you book a ticket to Cagliari. When—when are you thinking of going?'

'I don't know. Soon. I mean, I—don't know whether I will go.'

'Well, I'll—I'll ring Sophia just in case. That's the

maid. She speaks English by the way, and I've written her name and 'phone number down for you. She lives very near my house. She'll look after you, see that you have nothing to do. I'll—ring her and tell her she may or may not get a 'phone call from you. That's all you'll need to do if you decide to go. Ring Sophia the night before and she or her husband will meet you at the airport.' He looked at her carefully, saddened by her paleness, the pinched look about her face. 'I hope you go, darling. I think it's sensible. Have a good, long rest.'

She nodded, looking down at her hands because she was in danger of crying. 'Thank you. I'll—see that you get your keys back. Goodbye, Daniel.'

Goodbye? He heard the word but he refused utterly to believe it. She couldn't mean it. He had to give her time, that's all. Time to adjust to it all in her mind. God in heaven, she couldn't really be saying goodbye to him.

Could she?

'Donna, you've *got* to see that this, *all* of it, has nothing to do with us, *nothing at all*!'

'Hasn't it?'

'Donna! Look, if you'll just——'

'Go! Please leave me alone now. I can hardly think straight. Just—just *leave me alone*!'

Daniel got to his feet, making one last try. 'Can I come for you tomorrow? Siggy tells me you're being discharged.'

She forced herself to look at him, swallowing against the lump in her throat. 'Then he must also have told you that he's coming to take me home. Goodbye, Daniel.'

CHAPTER FIFTEEN

DONNA straightened up rather awkwardly from the task of packing her suitcase. She was doing it in her living room, having carried clothes downstairs a few at a time, knowing she would be unable to carry a full case down from her bedroom. It seemed illogical to her that they had not put any binding round her ribs while she was in hospital. They used to do that but these days it appeared that the medical profession deemed it better to leave them unbound, to leave nature to get on with the job of healing cracked ribs while the patient got on with life as best he or she could.

Which was precisely what she was doing, or trying to. She had been home for twenty-four hours and had rested, had slept like a log the previous night. This morning, apart from a troubled and tired mind, she was feeling much better, physically able to drive to her aunt and uncle's house in Rotherham. She needed to talk to them, she badly needed to tell them all that Daniel had told her about her father. There again there was the possibility that they already knew. Maybe they'd heard some gossip while they'd been at the house, looking after her. In any case she needed to discuss it with them, to see what they would say.

Right now, her overpowering feeling about the matter was anger. In her own eyes, her father was condemned. Not in any way could she reconcile his having an affair with Delia Conrad, most especially while his wife was alive. In fact she found it difficult to believe this was true. It wasn't that she doubted Daniel, she doubted Delia's word. After all, who else but she knew the entire truth? Joseph wasn't around to tell his tale and Delia might have tagged on a few years to the duration of the affair to make it all seem a little

155

more ... respectable, somehow, given that she'd been planning to divorce her husband. What kind of woman was she, anyway?

Donna did not intend to find out. She had no desire whatever to talk to Daniel's stepmother.

Gingerly, she hitched her suitcase to the floor and pushed it towards the front door. There was a very short distance between there and her Spitfire which was parked immediately outside, but the effort of lifting the case into the car made her break out in a sweat nevertheless.

She locked up her house and got into the driver's seat, panting a little and knowing a momentary anxiety at the prospect of driving. 'Come on, Donna,' she chided herself. 'Start the engine and get going. Accidents happen at the best of times, there's no need to lose your bottle.'

The police had questioned her about her accident, while she'd been in hospital. They were convinced she had skidded into the lamp-post but she still thought otherwise, at least if she had, it was because she'd fallen asleep at the wheel. Still, as the doctor had pointed out, it hardly mattered. She was alive, nobody else had been involved. Happily, Siggy's Mini was repairable and the insurance would take care of the expense.

One hour later she was racing along the motorway, as comfortable with her car as she had always been— except for the persistent protest from her rib-cage. She intended to have a good rest when she got to Rotherham, to stay with her relatives for at least a week. While she was there she intended also to drive over to Lincolnshire to visit her house, her old home. She had made an appointment with the tenants so she could do just that.

After that ... maybe she would go to Sardinia, she wasn't sure yet. She had the address and the keys to Daniel's villa in her handbag, together with her passport and her credit cards.

Daniel. The very thought of him added troubles to

her already troubled mind. He had not tried to contact her after her discharge from the hospital, nor did he know she was no longer at home but on her way to her aunt's. Donna hadn't even told Siggy where she was going, she'd said simply that she was going away to think. Siggy, loyal, faithful, as unquestioning as ever, had accepted this. As far as business was concerned there would be no problem. Today was the second of January and from now until the end of the month, there were no bookings. Siggy could cope with the shop, he had assured her of that. Apart from that, with the exception of his extracting a promise from her that she would take care of herself, he had said nothing at all.

It was a little after four when Donna pulled up on the short drive outside her aunt's semi-detached. It was in a cul-de-sac, a quiet spot, a three-bedroomed house with a nice guest-room in which Donna always felt at home.

'Donna!' Light spilled from the hallways as Aunt Liz threw open the front door. It was already dark, bitterly cold and Donna was shivering, tired and hungry. 'Come in, pet, come in! Oh, it's lovely to see you!'

Donna sidestepped her aunt, laughing a little and shaking her head as Elizabeth went automatically to hug her. 'The ribs, Auntie Liz, they're not up to it! Let's settle for a kiss, shall we? Ah, Uncle Desmond, I thought you'd be at work.'

'I've got a week off, plus the holiday.' Desmond, balding, middle-aged and kindly, appeared at the doorway of the living room and eyed his niece speculatively. 'Come here, chicken, let me take a good look at you. Can you imagine how worried we've been since we got your 'phone call last night? Why didn't you ring us from the hospital, why didn't you tell us you'd been in a car crash?'

'I did tell you, last night. Now don't fuss and don't worry any more. You can see for yourself that I'm fine.'

Her aunt and uncle exchanged looks, tut-tutting and not in the least comforted.

'What you need is a few days in bed.'

'What she needs is feeding up a bit!'

'You should have come to us on Christmas Eve, never mind going out to work.'

'It's high time there was something else in your life, besides that blasted shop of yours. Other girls of your age are interested in babies, not businesses.'

All that was fired at Donna before she'd even got in to the living room. Smiling inwardly, she nodded and took their criticisms with a straight face. It was good to see them, good to be here, and they meant well.

After four days with them, however, Donna was getting decidedly restless. Both her aunt and uncle were at home all day every day that week and the only privacy she got was when she was sleeping. She did a lot of that, she nodded off in the armchair by the roaring coal fire often, even against her will when she was watching something on the television.

Those four days proved to be just what she needed in that she was well-fed, fussed over and cared for by the only family she had. She was nearly twenty-five years old but for those few days she had reverted almost to the spoiled and pampered child she used to be. It did her the world of good and she was very grateful to her uncle and aunt, who in turn loved having her with them.

It was for this reason that she found it extremely difficult to broach the subject of her father and his affair with Delia Conrad. Uncle Desmond and Auntie Liz were—well, so obviously happy, contented, living quiet and uneventful lives which they wouldn't trade for the world, and Donna couldn't find it in her heart to upset them in any way. They would be upset, she knew, by her revelation, they would possibly be as angry as she was; they'd never got on terribly well with Joseph in any case, though they had come over to Lincolnshire to visit Alice Kent often in the past.

On the morning of her fifth day with them, Donna looked at her aunt and made what must have been her hundredth attempt to bring up that which was bothering her: did her aunt and uncle know already? Had Alice had any inkling of what her husband was up to? If so, had she confided in her sister? And if she had done that, what had her attitude been?

It was thoughts of her mother which were bothering Donna more than anything else. It was eating away at her, the idea that her mother, ill and frail as she was, might have known what her faithless husband had been up to. All those months, all those *years* before her death.

'Auntie Liz . . .' Aunt Liz was frying bacon and eggs while Uncle Desmond made a pot of tea and buttered the toast. Donna wasn't allowed to help. Outside, snow was falling, adding to the cosiness of the little breakfast nook in the kitchen and this seemed like as good a moment as any for Donna to make another attempt. 'I'm—going over to the Wolds tomorrow, to look over my house. Did I mention that to you?'

It was an oblique approach but at least it was a start.

'Yes, pet. You mentioned it on the 'phone, said you were thinking of selling the place.'

'That's right. I'm—not sure yet, though.'

Uncle Desmond looked up from his tasks. 'You should've sold the place years ago. Renting it hasn't been exactly profitable, has it? Mind you, the property itself has been as good as having money in the bank, it'll have increased in value.'

Donna fell silent, unsure how to carry on from here. 'I'm—it's—that house has always meant a lot to me, as you know. If I sell it, I'll be . . . sort of letting go of the past, if you see what I mean.'

'Of course we do.' Aunty Liz put an enormous breakfast before her, her eyes bright, her greying head nodding in approval. 'And a good thing, too.'

'What do you mean?' Donna looked at her swiftly, searching her eyes for a hint. 'Why is that a good thing?'

Elizabeth shrugged, blinking in surprise. 'Well, you lead your own life, you're happy in the south of

England—why bother keeping the house on? Come on, Des, I'm dishing up for you now.'

Nothing. There had been no ambiguity in her Aunt's words. Donna sighed inwardly, bracing herself for—she didn't know quite what. 'I—er—haven't told you this yet, but I met Daniel Conrad last June. At a party I was doing for a friend of his. It was—quite a coincidence, don't you think?'

This was met with blank looks. Donna repeated Daniel's name. 'Conrad, Daniel Conrad.'

Uncle Desmond made the connection first. 'Conrad, of course. The builders merchants in Lincoln. That's the chap your father bought his stuff from, isn't it? They were quite friendly, weren't they?'

Donna looked down at her plate, her appetite had vanished suddenly. She couldn't do it. It was glaringly obvious now that neither her aunt nor her uncle had had any inkling about the affair. 'No, you're thinking of Richard Conrad, Daniel's father. He—was a friend of Daddy's. Surely you haven't forgotten my father owed Conrads a great deal of money—that it was they who called the creditors' meeting that led to his bankruptcy?'

'Of course we haven't forgotten. The name had slipped my mind, that's all.'

Aunt Liz probed, sensing there was more to this. 'So what happened when you met Mr Conrad's son? I hope you were civil to him, Donna. I'd forgotten the name, too, but I haven't forgotten how bitter you were at the time, how you were convinced your dad had done away with himself. Thank goodness you soon got that notion out of your head, it's a terrible thought to have hanging over you.'

Donna looked from one pair of eyes to the other. Neither of them had known, of course, that she had nurtured this very notion for years and years. Almost seven of them. She saw her relatives too infrequently for them actually to know her, to know the woman she was today. Or rather, the woman she had been up until Christmas Day.

'Donna? What happened? When you met this Daniel? Did you recognise him straight away? What was he doing in the south, anyway?'

Did she recognise Daniel straight away? She smiled at the question, not bothering to answer it. 'He's moved down there. He has a transport company in Uxbridge now and a beautiful house in Chertsey, Surrey.'

Her relatives were exchanging looks again, smiling now, their ears pricking up almost visibly. 'Have you been going out with him then?'

'Is he a bachelor? How old is he?'

'Thirty-six, I think. He's—a widower, and yes, I've been going—going out with him.' Going out with him, it was a normal enough expression to use. But is that all it had been, her relationship with Daniel?

Aunt Liz was considering. 'Well, this is interesting, pet! Is he a nice person? Well, he must be if you've been spending time with him. Anyhow, I'm sure your father would have approved.'

That did it. Donna put her knife and fork down, her food only half eaten. The irony in her aunt's last remark almost choked her. Joseph Conrad would have approved. Dear Lord, it was enough to make the mind boggle.

She stuck her chin in the palm of her hand and resigned herself to the conclusion that it would be utterly pointless to tell them about the affair. They couldn't help her, she couldn't learn anything from them, it would serve only to upset them needlessly.

A plan was forming in her mind. While Aunt Liz fussed about the uneaten breakfast, Donna was thinking ahead. It was time to go, she had been here long enough.

'Anyway,' she said brightly, making an effort to finish her breakfast. 'What I was going to tell you is that Daniel has a house in Sardinia and he's invited me to go over for a while, to recuperate, you know. He thinks I need a good, long rest.'

'He's right there,' Uncle Desmond said grimly.

'You're still as pale as I don't know what. Some sea air would do you the world of good.'

Aunt Liz clearly had her doubts. 'You mean, you're going to stay with him—alone? In his house? Well, I'm sorry if I sound a bit old-fashioned but I'm not sure your father would have approved of *that*. Nor would your mother.'

With a brave smile which she hoped would keep the threat of tears at bay, Donna shook her head. Bless your heart, Aunt Liz, she thought, bless your old-fashioned innocence. 'No, I wouldn't be staying alone with Daniel, of course not. Much as you call me a modern girl and think I'm far too independent, I do have certain rules of my own. I'm going to Sardinia alone. As a matter of fact, I think I'll go on Saturday if I can get a flight. I'll ring the airline this afternoon.'

Donna made two telephone calls that afternoon. Fortunately her aunt and uncle went shopping and made no objection when she declined to go with them. She had the house and the telephone to herself. She did manage to get a flight for Saturday, from Gatwick, though she was told she would have to fly firstly to Bologna and stay the night before catching a connecting flight to Sardinia, not that she minded this.

The second telephone call was one she made because she felt she had no choice but to do so. Not any more. She simply had to get some answers, most especially to the question which was now beginning to keep her awake at night. She absolutely did not want to talk to the woman, to see her, but she needed to, she *had* to. So she made an appointment . . . an *assignation*, with her father's mistress for the afternoon on Friday.

Tomorrow was Thursday.

The drive was covered with snow. It lay inches deep, covering bushes and trees in the garden, shapes and bumps which were both familiar and unfamiliar to her.

Donna got out of her car and left it parked at the foot of the drive. She wanted to walk the rest of the way to her house, to cover the distance slowly, to see how it made her feel, being back here.

The house looked exactly the same, its white, pebble-dash façade looking perhaps rather dull thanks to the grey, heavily overcast sky. Snow was still falling gently, floating down through an almost windless atmosphere.

Nothing. She wasn't feeling anything.

She had got almost as far as the front door when two children appeared, coming round the corner of the house. They were pushing a huge ball of snow and they stopped in their tracks, looking at Donna with curiosity.

'Mummy's in the kitchen.'

'Are you the lady who brings that scent in pretty boxes?'

Donna stifled a smile. The question had come from a girl aged about six or seven, the statement about Mummy from a boy who was a little older. 'No, I'm ...' What should she say? I'm the lady who owns this house? 'I'm ... your landlady.'

'What's a landlady?'

'Shut up, twit.' The boy intervened, being very superior and grown up. 'I knew you were coming. Mummy's been tidying up all morning, she made me clear up my room.'

'Well, I'm—sorry about that.' She laughed openly. Out of the mouths of babes. 'Which room is yours?'

'The one with the chestnut tree outside it, at the back.'

Donna nodded. So this little boy was sleeping in what used to be her bedroom. She looked from him to his sister and within minutes she had been invited to see their rooms, to see the toys they'd been given for Christmas.

'I thought I heard voices! Now, what are you two up to?' A tall, black haired man appeared in the doorway, striding outside quickly as he spotted Donna, proffering his hand. 'You must be Miss Kent. Michael MacDonald.'

Donna shook hands with her tenant, the first one she had ever met in person. Michael MacDonald hailed from Edinburgh, he was an architect and he had supplied to Donna's estate agents impeccable references when he'd taken on the house some eighteen months earlier. That was all she knew about him except that she liked him on sight.

'Sorry about those two,' he grinned, nodding towards his children. 'Keeping you chatting in this weather. There's another one inside, my twelve year old! Come and meet him and my wife. She's got the kettle on, you must be ready for a hot drink. Foul weather, isn't it?'

Mrs MacDonald and her twelve year old son were just as warm and friendly as the others. Donna was given a guided tour of the house she had lived in for so many years; it was a curious experience for her, very curious.

The lady of the house might have had a frantic tidy-up that morning but this in no way indicated neglect on her part. The house was spotless, impressive with the kind of remotest-corner-cleanliness which could not be achieved by a quick whip-round two hours before a visitor called. No, the house was well cared for, even loved by those who were living in it. Not only was Donna told this verbally, she could see it for herself.

It did not look like her house, the house she remembered, despite much of the furniture being her own. She was told that the MacDonald's had a lot of their own belongings in storage, that they'd had to do that because they were unable to find a suitable unfurnished house. Some of their possessions were around, though, several paintings on the ground and upper floors, lamps and lamp standards, cushions, a rug here and there. It was more than enough to make Donna feel that this was someone else's house, not hers.

Or was it?

Perhaps it was simply that she wasn't feeling anything, not feeling any emotional attachment. It surprised her. It also relieved her, in a way. Of what, she couldn't be sure.

'The swing. Where's—what happened to the swing that was out there?' Standing by the window in the little boy's bedroom, Donna looked down into the garden, her question coming idly. She wasn't really concerned about the swing, she was thinking back through the years, seeing herself in the garden on a summer's day. Even as a teenager she had used her swing. Her father had installed it for her when she was very young, yet she could still recall her parents' fuss as to whether it were properly secured. She closed her eyes briefly, sighing without realising she was doing so. Had they been as happy as she had always believed them to be? How *could* they have been?

'I'm sorry about that,' Mr MacDonald was saying. 'It was falling to pieces, quite dangerous. There was no point in storing it away for you, it was very rusty and—well, frankly it was useless. We threw it out.'

At the hint of apology in his voice, Donna smiled. 'Quite right, too.'

'Daddy's going to put up a swing for us in the spring,' his daughter piped up. 'If we stay here, that is. Can we stay here?'

'We've looked at lots of other houses,' her younger brother added. 'But we don't like any of them as much as we like this one. We want to stay here. Are you going to sell it to us?'

'Behave yourself,' his mother scolded. 'You might be embarrassing Miss Kent with your questions.'

'No, no, that's all right.' Donna's eyes moved slowly around the room. Gone was the pink and white flowery wallpaper she had once adored. There were aeroplanes on the walls now. In the corner where once had lived her array of dolls and teddies, an electric train set stood and behind the bedroom door on which there had once been a life-size photograph of her latest heart-throb there was now a picture of a pop group whose name she didn't even know.

Her eyes came to rest on the rather serious twelve

year old who had been standing, saying nothing. 'And what about you, Daniel, do you like the house?'

'David,' he corrected. 'My name's David. 'Yes, I love it. It's a bit like the one we had in Scotland, before Daddy changed his job.'

Donna looked straight at the man in question. 'Well, Mr MacDonald, if you're still interested in buying, shall we go downstairs and discuss the price?'

CHAPTER SIXTEEN

THE hotel room was impersonal, probably the best place for her meeting with Daniel's stepmother. She had considered meeting her in the bar but had decided against it; in here there would be complete privacy. The venue had in fact been Delia's suggestion and it suited Donna nicely, the hotel being just outside Sleaford, some miles south of Lincoln. She had taken a room for the night and would drive down to Gatwick first thing in the morning, to catch the late afternoon flight to Sardinia, via Bologna. Perhaps there she would get some peace, be able to restore her mind and body to normality.

She stood by the window, watching the snow which was falling yet again, it was billowing about wildly in the wind this afternoon, making the roads hazardous but by no means impassable.

With her arms folded across her chest, she stood, her stomach knotted with anger and apprehension, her fingers resting lightly against her still tender ribs. She was dressed in black to suit her mood, in a plain woollen sweater dress with a polo neck, its severity broken only by the simple gold chain she was wearing. It was important to her that she looked impeccable, her make-up had been applied carefully and a little more heavily than usual. She did not want to look pale or frail in Delia Conrad's eyes. Apart from her fringe, her hair was scraped back from her face into a tight knot on the crown. She moved from the window and took another look at herself in the mirror, glancing at her watch as she crossed the room. It was ten past twelve. Twenty minutes. There were still twenty minutes to go before the wretched woman was due.

Wretched woman? Yes, *yes*! She closed her eyes,

murmuring softly to herself in the stillness of the room. 'Oh, Daniel! What a mess, what an unholy mess! Here I am, waiting to see the woman who was, is, a mother to you, the woman who brought you up since you were nine years old.' And I hate her, she added silently. I hate her before she's even got here, before she's spoken even one word to me.

When the telephone shrilled, Donna snatched up the receiver anxiously and sat on the side of the bed, her legs feeling suddenly weak. 'Yes?' It was reception, telling her that a lady was asking for her. Her visitor was fifteen minutes early. 'Send—ask her to come up to my room, please.'

Donna stood, smoothing down the skirt of her dress. She looked swiftly around the room. Of course it was spotless, none of her belongings were in sight. In the corner there was a small, circular table flanked by two chairs upholstered in fawn tweed. They could sit there to talk.

How was she going to be civil to the woman? How could she hold back her resentment sufficiently to hold a conversation with her when every time she thought of her mother she would want to spit in Delia Conrad's eye?

Daniel, she moaned silently, why did it have to be your stepmother? If it had to be someone, why someone so close to you? Moreover, why did it have to be Daniel she had fallen in love with? Why, when this had happened to her for the first time in her life, did it have to be with him? Worse still, why did she have to love him, too? Why couldn't it simply be a case of being *in* love, that sort of transient state when one knows from experience—other peoples' if not one's own—that one will get over it?

But no, it wasn't merely that. God knew she had spent enough time thinking, in the hospital and while she'd been resting at her aunt's, to realise she loved Daniel very much and had done for a long time. He had been right all along in saying she resented him. She had.

And it was this, this illogical resentment, that had stopped her from admitting her feelings for him even to herself. Though he had been exonerated of something he had not been responsible for in the first place, she had still resented him. Of *course* it didn't make sense, it never had, but she had felt constantly that she was being somehow disloyal to the memory of her father by even seeing Daniel. Yet she had been unable to give him up. She had, as she realised now, fallen in love with him, grown to love him deeply, *against her will*. How ludicrous that seemed in the light of what she'd recently learned, in the face of her father's own disloyalty!

Her current overriding and contradictory thoughts didn't make sense, either: she wished fervently that Daniel had never told her about her father and she wished just as strongly that he had told her about it when she was eighteen.

If he had told her then, her life from the age of eighteen onwards might have been entirely different. Dammit, yes, yes, yes, he had been right in saying that her thinking her father committed suicide had been the main reason for her working so hard, her absolute single-mindedness, for feeling unworthy of being loved, for her missing out on her youth . . . for her missing so much laughter and sunshine through the intervening years. It had been that, plus the gossip which had angered her so, plus the supposed stigma attached to her name, plus her fierce and stupid pride, plus her crazy attachment to her childhood home, her attachment to the past. And it was, *all of it*, based on misconceptions, false premises, events, memories and ideas which weren't *real* in the first place.

God in heaven, talk about disillusionment! Talk about a rude awakening!

But she was awake now, awake, aware and very sure of what she wanted to do with her life from now on, very sure. The trouble was that when she did what she wanted to do, Daniel was going to find himself with yet another problem on his hands.

She stiffened, catching her breath as she heard the tapping at her door. It was a small sound, light and very brief, not the knock of someone who was feeling confident.

Pleased by this, given confidence herself by it, Donna headed for the door. It was for Daniel's sake alone that she was going to try very, very hard to be civil during this exchange. Delia was, after all, his stepmother.

She opened the door to see a face, a woman, who was instantly recognisable if only because of the striking red hair she remembered so well, but that was all she remembered. Having met her only once and many years ago at that, when she herself was a young teenager and had taken little notice of the woman, what shocked Donna now was Delia Conrad's comparative youth. Knowing Daniel's age and thinking about this woman lately, Donna had imagined her to be at least in her middle fifties, a few years older than her father would have been had he lived. She wasn't. She couldn't have been more than ten years older than Daniel and she could easily pass for forty.

Tall, slender, straight-backed, Delia Conrad looked elegant in a dark green three-quarter length coat with a matching skirt. The coat was a swingy style, flaring into an A line and trimmed with fur, mink to be precise, and in one hand she held a black leather bag and gloves. Her hair was short and softly styled, precisely the shade it had always been with not even a hint of grey in it. The colour was natural, too, which was something else that startled Donna now. Her make up was immaculate, just a little dramatic yet not overdone, and she looked at Donna with eyes which were quite vividly green, smiling uncertainly but enough to reveal nice, even teeth.

'I'm—early,' she said, her own nervousness apparent in her hesitation, in the tone of her voice, in the fact that behind her make-up, her face was pale.

'Yes.' Donna turned away, ignoring the outstretched hand, feeling unnerved by the woman's appearance. She was really quite beautiful even now, she must have been stunning when she was younger. 'Come in, Mrs Conrad. We have met, just once, some years ago.'

Delia closed the door and followed her into the room. 'We've met several times, Donna, once when you were four and your father had you shake hands with me properly, as he put it, then again when you were about seven, when Richard and I came to your house. You were just going to bed and you were having a little tantrum——'

'All right!' Donna spoke sharply, the knot in her stomach tightening against the unexpected warmth in the other woman's voice. She found this meeting, the entire scene, distasteful. But it was necessary, for *her*. She was hoping it would give her some peace of mind . . . but she wasn't going to get very far if she continued as she'd begun.

'Please sit down, Mrs Conrad.' She strove to be civil, for Daniel's sake. He had urged her to have this meeting; it was important to him, too, that Donna got some answers. 'I—won't keep you long. All I want of you are some straightforward answers to some straightforward questions.' She waited, watching the play of expressions on the other woman's face. She saw fear, she saw disappointment and sorrow very clearly.

'Won't you sit down, too, Donna? You're making me nervous, looking at me like that, and you look as tense as I feel.'

Choosing the foot of the bed rather than the other chair, happier because it put more distance between them, Donna sat. Calmly, unnaturally so, she put her first and most important question, her eyes monitoring Delia's still pale face. 'I want to know, I need to know, whether my mother knew about your affair with Daddy. It's important to me and I must have the truth——'

Obviously shocked at the idea, Delia looked horrified. 'Of course not, of *course* not! Your father loved your mother, make no mistake about that.'

Donna didn't even bother to answer that one.

'I'm—can't we be civilised about this? Please. For Daniel's sake, if not our own. I—Donna, from what he's told me, there's every chance that I'm going to be your mother-in-law one day.'

'Just explain about Mummy, I don't want to hear anything else. For all you know, my mother might have known about you and put up with it, suffered in silence. One thing's for sure, she would have suffered, it would have hurt her terribly because on the day she died she was as potty about my father as she had been on the day she married him. She said so often and it was plain for a blind man to see. She was utterly devoted to him. Of course, fool that I am, I'd have said the same thing about *him*! I only wish I *could* say the same for him! So what do I know, really? What the hell is real in this life?'

Delia looked down at her hands. There was so much, so very much she wanted to say to this girl, this lovely girl who was Joseph's daughter, his only child. If she could be given the chance to explain it, all of it, she could make Donna understand, she was sure she could. But she wasn't going to be given that chance, and the realisation made her tremble inside. Apart from her own desire to help, Daniel was going to be very disappointed, not that he knew this meeting was taking place. Delia had not 'phoned to tell him because she hadn't wanted to raise his hopes. But he was banking on her to clear this thing up if she got the chance, to tell Donna personally the things she had told him in confidence, when seven years ago there had been all that trouble and heartbreak, when she had had to justify herself both to Daniel and to his sister or else risk losing the closeness they had always had as a family. She had made them both understand, both adults who were her children, regardless of ages, blood-ties or anything else.

Not for a very long time would she be able to tell her this, maybe she would never be able to tell her, but she loved Donna, she loved her not only because she was

Joseph's flesh and blood, not only because she was so precious to her beloved son, but also because she did in fact know her quite well. She knew her because Joseph had talked so much about her, she knew her because she, too, had once been her age and riddled with regrets and confusion. She knew her because she knew she loved Daniel.

But Delia said nothing, she didn't move.

The silence was broken by Donna, sighing deeply and mentally telling herself off for her lack of control. 'Mrs Conrad, I—would you ... Look, I'm sorry. I'd—I would like to talk more. Can you? I mean, will Richard be wondering where you are? He doesn't know where you are, does he?'

'No, I've told him I'm having lunch and then going shopping with a friend. There was no point at all in his knowing——'

'Yes, yes, I see that. I'll ring down for some coffee. I should have done that before but I wasn't thinking ...'

The older woman smiled gratefully. 'Maybe you could even manage to call me Delia?'

The following few minutes were awkward. Both women were trying to compose themselves, making an effort, feeling unsure of one another. Donna rang down for coffee, Delia having declined the offer of sandwiches, then she sat quietly while Delia went into the bathroom.

Delia took off her coat when she emerged, having tidied her face while trying frantically to put her thoughts into some semblance of order. She sat, glancing swiftly at Donna, who was on the edge of the bed again, looking white-faced and very strained. 'I'm really very sorry about your accident, Donna. It was a shock when Daniel got that 'phone call, he—we had no idea how bad your injuries were then, your employee didn't know at that point. I understand it was his Mini van you were driving? You can imagine how Daniel felt, he was frantic ...' Her voice trailed off as room service came with the coffee. 'I'll get it.'

'I'll pour, shall I?' Delia went ahead, deliberately placing the cup on the table in the hope that Donna would come and sit by her. She did.

There was a long silence before Delia plunged in. 'I—was seeing your father for five years in all. Right up to his death. I—I wanted to marry him, Donna.'

Donna was staring into her cup, working out the implications of what might have been. 'How hilarious,' she said dully, 'Daniel and I might have had the same stepmother.'

Silence again.

'You—can't have seen Daddy often?' Donna asked at length, her curiosity getting the better of her. 'I believe you were very discreet and——'

'We saw each other two or three times a month. It wasn't difficult, Joseph being self-employed and having no fixed routine, my being free all day. We met out of town, miles away from our respective homes, at different places. It—it did start as a purely sexual thing——'

Donna's head came up. 'I don't want that kind of detail, please spare me that part of it.'

'You've got to hear it. That *was* part of it, certainly in the beginning. You need all the parts to make up a whole. And I want you to see the whole picture, Donna, so bear with me and let me explain.'

She paused, sighing heavily because she hardly knew where to start. This was excruciatingly difficult. 'Bear in mind that you were just thirteen when my affair with your father began, you were only eighteen when he died. I know how close you were to your parents, both of them, and how close they were, but there are things you couldn't have known. The sexual side of their marriage——' Delia stopped again, faltered then said it rapidly. It had to be said. 'I'm talking about when your father was about thirty-seven, thirty-eight, bear that in mind, too. He was a normal, healthy man and your mother—well, you know the state of her health. That side of their marriage—this is something you would

never have given a moment's thought to, something I
didn't learn about for some time, obviously. But it's
very relevant because Joseph and I—well, we had been
physically attracted from the moment we'd met, years
earlier. Throughout those years nothing had been said
between us, it was just—there. Nothing at all happened
for many years.

'In the early days, I mean when we—when we first
started seeing each other, it was understood very clearly
by both of us that it was leading nowhere. You see,
Donna, we both loved our spouses, we were both happy
with our marriages. Can you believe that, Donna? Will
you believe it?'

'Yes,' came the quiet reply. 'I know my father was
happy with my mother.' She met Delia's eyes steadily.
'What about you? I mean, I hadn't realised until today
how young you are. Your husband must be much older
than you.'

'I'm forty-nine now. Richard is seventy.'

'Seventy?' Donna frowned. Of course, he must be
about that, she hadn't really registered ... 'You—
Delia, you're only thirteen years older than Daniel!'

There was a smile, a genuine smile. 'Daniel was nine
when I married his father. I was twenty-two. Richard
was forty-three.' The smile faded. 'I worked at Conrad's
in those days, that's how I met Richard. I'd been there
only three months when he asked me to marry him, I'd
been out with him barely a dozen times. But I was in
love with him, crazy about him. The age gap didn't
enter into my thinking. In fact, I didn't think at all
about what I was doing. I was too much in love. There
was ... well, maybe Richard was something of a father
figure to me. I'd never really known my father. I'd
never been married, I'd never made love with anyone,
never even been involved with a man in any serious
way—and Richard swept me off my feet. He thought I
was the most beautiful woman alive, he showered me
with gifts and ... and all of that influenced me greatly.
I'd never had anything, you see, material things, I

mean. I had no family to speak of. My parents had divorced years earlier and I'd lost track of my father. I'd lived with my mother until I left home at eighteen. I was born in Sheffield, my mother still lives there.'

Donna didn't interrupt. Delia had strayed far from the point but that no longer mattered. She was being honest. There was a wistfulness about her now, a sadness in her eyes as she looked into her past. What mattered to Donna, though, was the woman's honesty. She had been influenced by the things Richard could offer her and she was admitting as much. 'But you were in love with him when you married him?'

'Oh, God, yes.' The words came without vehemence, without drama. 'Very much so. And I thought his children adorable, I've always loved children.'

'But you never had any of your own. Why is that?'

Delia smiled again, shaking her head a little. It was a sad smile. 'Richard refused to. Oh, Donna, there's so much . . .' She fell silent, looking at Donna helplessly. 'You see, I—well, I've just told you I didn't think about what I was doing. I married Richard without taking into account our age difference. He was twice my age, he'd been married to his first wife for fifteen years and he had all the family he'd ever wanted. He had a son and a daughter and he didn't want any more. I tried for years to talk him round. Then when I was thirty and starting to panic, when my wanting children became a source of real trouble between us, I realised that it wasn't just selfishness on Richard's part, he felt that he was too old to start another family, to cope with young children again. He was also a bit frightened because his first wife had died in childbirth.'

'Oh, yes, I'd forgotten that. But Daniel did tell me. Nevertheless, I think it was selfish of him, very. Would he have considered adopting?'

'*I* wouldn't consider adopting. Donna, I already had two children who weren't my own. I mean, I loved them dearly, make no mistake, but they weren't——'

'I understand,' Donna interrupted. 'So you couldn't talk Richard round?'

'No. No way. God knows I tried to.'

'But you still wanted to be married to him at that point?'

'Heavens, yes! Don't misunderstand, Donna. This was a bone of contention between us for many years but I resigned myself to it eventually. There were many things Richard and I should have discussed before we married—but we didn't. Consequently I didn't really know him when I married him. Do you see what I mean? But I didn't regret it, I honestly mean that. In every other respect he was a marvellous husband, a good father, too. I couldn't fault him. I was no longer *in* love with him, his attitude towards my having children cured me of that. But I loved him. By then I loved him as I hadn't loved him when I married him, I was merely in love with him then. Do you understand? There's a difference, you know, Donna. All the difference in the world.'

It was Donna's turn to smile. 'That much, I have discovered. There's—I suppose the ideal is when a couple have both?' She wanted an answer to this. It seemed obvious but she wanted to know what Delia thought.

'Absolutely, absolutely.' Delia was pleased, delighted. So far, so good. Very good. 'And it's this,' she ventured, watching the younger woman closely, 'that your father and I had. What started as a physical attraction turned very rapidly into that state of euphoria people refer to as being in love. That was a very, very, difficult time for us both. There was the temptation to meet more often, to take risks and see each other as much as we possibly could. But we didn't. We continued to meet infrequently because of the risks involved. Neither of us wanted to hurt our partners. As time went on, Joseph told me very clearly that he loved your mother, that he would never leave her, and I loved him for that. I respected it. I loved him very, very much,

Donna, and I only wish . . .' She couldn't go on. Her eyes flooded with tears and she was fumbling in her bag again. 'I'm sorry. I'm sorry.'

'It's all right.' Donna looked away, feeling guilty at Delia's fast and profuse apology for crying. She had no idea that Donna was fighting the threat of tears herself.

'I wish, I *wish* I'd known that all these years you've been thinking he killed himself. Believe me, if I had I'd have come looking for you and told you everything myself. You see, on the day Joseph died, he was on his way to meet me. I'd spoken to him on the 'phone that morning and he told me he'd been up all night, wrestling with figures, as he put it. You know the financial trouble he was in and—he'd been half out of his mind with worry. Donna, my guess is that he nodded off at the wheel. It happens, you know, it only needs a moment——'

Without warning, Donna burst into tears. 'Oh, God! Oh, God!' That was all she could say through her sobs. It was the truth. This was how he died. She just knew it, not only because there was no alternative explanation but because . . . because it just *felt* like the truth.

Delia watched and waited. More than anything in the world she wanted to take Donna into her arms and comfort her. But she dared not, she dared not approach her physically. She kept still and she kept quiet until the girl recovered.

'I—that's what happened to me, Delia! The police say I skidded on ice but I think I fell asleep at the wheel. I'd been working . . . it doesn't matter,' she finished dully. 'Go on, Delia. How did it get to the stage when you were prepared to leave your husband?'

'It was partly Joseph's bankruptcy, partly because he needed me and——'

'About that. Didn't Richard have an ulterior motive for what he did?'

'No. He knew nothing at that stage. That was business pure and simple. Neither personalities nor anything else came into it. Of course, I was as upset as your father. I, too, resented Richard for being the instigator of your father's bankruptcy—illogical though I knew it was. But that resentment was part of—of everything coming to a head, I suppose, in my marriage. Alice had died eighteen months earlier, your father wanted to marry me—but he didn't push it. Richard was unwell and had been for some time, with ulcer trouble.

'Joseph knew I still loved my husband, in a different way by then, and he didn't press me to leave him, he didn't ask me to do something he himself wouldn't have done—leave your mother.

'That was the sort of love your father and I had, Donna. That was the relationship we shared, and not for one moment do I regret what we had together.' Unconsciously, Delia's head lifted as she looked straight at the younger woman. 'I make no apology.'

Donna smiled slightly, respecting Delia for that. What could she say after all she had learned? 'What happened in the end, Delia? How did Richard find out about the affair?'

'I told him, of course. I finally made up my mind to leave him, to marry your father. Regardless of everything. Joseph needed me as he had never needed me before. Richard much less so. His children were adults, Suzie was already married and Daniel was on the brink of it. Richard was still head of his precious company, still working as many hours as he always had and ... and I still had half a lifetime ahead of me. I thought Joseph had, too. Oh, Lord ...'

Delia reached blindly for Donna's hand. It was already there, on the table, reaching for hers.

'There's a little more, Donna, just a little more. Your father was in quite a state. It would have passed, he would have bounced back, it was all due to his financial trouble. He got drunk from time to time, during those awful weeks. He once called me from a pub, some pub, I don't remember what it was called. It was on his side of Lincoln, some miles from his house.

Anyhow, he 'phoned my house and he was very maudlin, blind drunk, so much so, he didn't even realise what a chance he was taking in phoning me. I was terrified for him in case he attempted to drive home. I slipped out of the house immediately and went in search of him.

'He'd gone when I got to the pub. I've just remembered its name, it was called the Hare and Hounds and it seems Joseph had been going there quite a lot. When I asked for him, I was in quite a state myself and I was told that a taxi had taken him home. As I turned away from the bar I saw someone who knew Richard and me quite well. I knew also that that person heard me enquiring about your father. That's where the gossip started, Donna. It can only be that. I know we were never actually seen together.'

Exhausted, drained, Delia got to her feet. 'It was then that I told Richard I was leaving. That very night, when I got home. It was awful,' she added hurriedly, embarrassed now. 'He wept and he begged me to stay, he blamed himself for his selfishness. I had never thought he'd take it so hard. He told Daniel and Suzie, and for two weeks I—I went through hell. I faltered, torn between my husband and Joseph, and still Joseph put no pressure on me.'

She picked up her coat, her shoulders slumped as she turned back to look at Donna. 'I was leaving Richard. Your father died believing that, believing I was going to marry him. What he didn't know, which is perhaps just as well——' She broke off suddenly, staring at nothing.

'What?' Donna got up quickly. 'Delia, are you all right? What is it? What didn't Daddy know?'

Delia looked at her oddly, as though she were not really there, as though she were talking to herself. 'That I probably would never have left Richard. Fate stepped in. Fate, or something. Retribution maybe. I don't know. On the evening before your father died, Richard took ill, dangerously ill. His ulcer burst and he was rushed into hospital. This is the reason I 'phoned 'oseph the following morning. I was calm enough but I old him nothing. I didn't want to tell him over the phone so I asked him to meet me. He didn't know here was anything amiss, he didn't think it odd. We ixed a time and a place and—and I was going to tell im I couldn't walk out on Richard when he was so ill. —it's—you know the rest.'

'Delia——'

'I have to go. It's almost four and I must get back.'

'Stay, please. Just give me ten minutes more. It's— here are one or two things I want to say to you.'

Hope flared in the older woman's eyes. 'We can meet omorrow.'

'No, I'm afraid we can't. I'm driving to Gatwick first hing, I'm flying to Sardinia, going to stay in Daniel's iouse there for a few weeks.'

'A few weeks . . .?' The hope faded and died.

Delia stayed, just for another ten minutes.

Ten minutes, time enough in which to complete their exchange.

CHAPTER SEVENTEEN

It was snowing again the following morning. Donna looked at it despairingly from the hotel window. It was dawn, just, but she had already been up for an hour drinking tea and thinking, thinking, thinking.

She wanted to leave straight away but she was going to do the sensible thing and get a good, hot breakfast inside her before she set off. The drive ahead of her was a long one and last night, after Delia had gone, she had completely forgotten to have dinner. Instead she had trudged out into the snow and had walked for miles, unable to stay cooped up any longer in the hotel bedroom.

She had got back around nine, feeling cold but very much at peace. At last. During her long walk she had finally sorted everything out in her mind. This morning's thinking had been exclusively about her business and what she was going to do with it.

After bathing and dressing, she looked at her watch. It would be all right to ring Siggy now. It was Saturday, he would be up and working already. She picked up the receiver and dialled direct. 'Siggy? Hello, darling, it's me. I'm—you see . . .' Suddenly she didn't quite know how to tell him. 'Siggy, have you got a few minutes . . .?'

A little later, after breakfast in the hotel dining room, Donna packed her suitcase and checked her watch again. She could ring the airline now.

The airline took ages to answer and she waited patiently on their queueing system, listening to music which was being piped over the 'phone, supposedly to prevent one getting bored while waiting to hear a human voice. Every now and then a recorded voice would interrupt, explaining that the lines were still engaged, then the music would come back.

At last she was put through. 'Ah, yes, my name's Kent, Donna Kent. I'm booked on this afternoon's flight from Gatwick to Bologna and I'm ringing——'

She was interrupted, assured that all flights were leaving the airport, that the weather was not affecting departures. 'No, no, I'm not concerned about that, I'm ringing to cancel my seat. No, I'm not concerned about a refund, either . . .'

At nine twenty-five she took a last look around the room and had a porter come up for her case while she went downstairs to pay her bill.

By noon she was halfway to Surrey. To Chertsey, to be precise. She was on her way to Daniel. She was going home.

'Thank God for that!' he'd said last night, when after her walk she had 'phoned him and made the announcement without preamble. 'Oh, Donna, I can't tell you how much I've missed you! Where have you been all this time? I knew you weren't in Sardinia because I've been ringing there half a dozen times a day. Darling, where are you now? More importantly, how are you?'

The warmth, the enthusiasm, the tenderness in his voice had brought tears to her eyes, a constriction in her throat which made speech impossible for the moment. 'I'm in a hotel near Sleaford. I'm—oh, Daniel, you ask how I am? I'm . . . I'm a little older and a lot wiser. I—oh, darling, I've got so much to say to you I can't wait till I see you. But it's late now, it's pitch dark and I'm tired, I just can't face the drive right now.'

There was a momentary silence before Daniel's quiet, Darling? That is what you called me, isn't it, Donna?'

'Yes,' she said softly, 'because that's what you are to me. I'll get to you as fast as I possibly can tomorrow.'

'No!' All tenderness was suddenly gone. 'You will drive *slowly*, young lady. You will take great care and you will drive slowly and get to me without incident. And Donna . . . get a good night's sleep now. And

Donna,' he added, his tone changing again so she could hear the smile in his voice. 'I love you.'

Now, she drove carefully as instructed, Donna smiled to herself at the memory of that brief conversation. It had been mean of her not to tell him she loved him in return, silly perhaps that she wanted to wait so she could see his face when she said those words to him for the first time.

The journey seemed interminable. The motorway was boring, the traffic moving by no means more slowly than normal, in spite of the weather. Donna kept up with it, but she was taking care. She had no intention of having another accident.

At one o'clock she pulled into a service area and filled up with petrol, tempted to press on with her journey but allowing common sense to dictate for the second time that day. It made a change. She went into the cafeteria and had a cup of coffee, a sandwich and a rest. Her ribs were still tender but they were getting less painful by the day. Time would heal them. Didn't time heal all things?

Who had said that? In her opinion the answer was no, time didn't heal all things, it merely dulled them or allowed one eventually to put things into perspective. Or it enabled one to accept. Yes, the passage of time did enable one to accept that what was done was done and, though there might be regrets, there was no changing what was in the past.

Nobody's past could be changed, but Donna was thinking about her own in particular. She could only learn from it, from the good times as well as the bad. But the most important lesson she had learned was that the past had shaped her present. Likewise, the present would shape her future. She was going to enjoy the present, the here and now and all that she had. For seven years she had existed in some sort of emotional limbo, she hadn't really *lived* at all. Well, all that was over now. She had changed and she was going to enjoy the present but she was also going to bear in mind how it would affect her future.

She had learned quite a few things from Delia
onrad.

When she got north of London the traffic was dense,
ough the snow had thinned out considerably
ompared to what it had been in the Midlands. By the
me she reached Surrey, however, it was snowing again,
ut, now, it was suddenly beautiful rather than
azardous.

She turned into Daniel's drive a little after four. It
as already dark and the house looked welcoming,
oming large before her with lights blazing from every
indow. She laughed aloud, knowing Daniel had done
is deliberately.

He was out the front door and opening the car for
er before she'd even brought it to a halt. Still laughing,
e greeted him with, 'You idiot! All those lights, think
the electricity bill!' She climbed out of the low-slung
pitfire, aided by Daniel's firm grip on her arm. 'The
ace looks like a beacon shining in the——'

It was curious how it didn't hurt when he put his
ms around her, when he held her closely as he cut off
r words with a long, lingering kiss.

'Night!' she giggled, when he finally raised his head.

'Donna! Oh, my darling Donna!' She couldn't know
, but her big blue eyes were shining brightly, too. They
ere lit with love—and that's all the illumination
aniel needed right now. He put one hand on either
de of her face and kissed her over and over again, on
r nose, on her mouth, her cheeks, her closed eyelids.

Oblivious to the falling snow, as he was, Donna slid
er arms tightly around his neck, resting her head
gainst his shoulder as he held her closely but tenderly.

Weariness had caught up with her, weariness from
e drive, from the emotions of yesterday. 'Daniel,
elia didn't 'phone you last night, did she?'

'No, darling.' He spoke against her hair, his lips
rushing over the top of her ear.

'No. Good. She said she wouldn't, I asked her to
ave that to me.'

Daniel stiffened, holding her at arm's length so h
could see her face. 'You've talked to her?' He looke
alarmed, suddenly unsure—of Donna, of everythin
'Donna, why didn't you say? When was this? What—
happened?'

She just smiled, watching those changeable eyes of h
turn from hazel to something a fraction darker. Ther
were snowflakes on his dark blond head, he wasn't eve
wearing a jacket. 'Are we going to stand out here a
night?'

'Donna, please! What—how did it go?'

'Put it this way,' she said simply, unable to take he
eyes from his. God, he was beautiful! Why had sh
never thought him beautiful before? He was, big an
beautiful. 'Your stepmother is a very special lady. I lik
her. I couldn't help liking her. We—oh, Daniel, there
so much to tell you but for the moment, just let m
apologise.'

'For what? To whom?'

'To you, of course. I've been so stupid and—and eve
up to yesterday I was planning to go away for a fe
weeks. But after talking to Delia ... you see, oh, dea
you'll think me such an idiot. Days ago, I made up m
mind to marry you, to come back to you, but I though
there was going to be a problem. For you. I thought I'
have to tell you that if we married, I would never, eve
have any contact at all with your parents, whic
wouldn't have been very nice for you. So I thought I'
go away and think this over—and take the rest you'
insisted I take. But now ...'

'But now? *What?*' In his anxiety at what might b
coming, Daniel forgot her cracked ribs. He caught hol
of her, as though terrified suddenly that he hadn't wo
her yet.

'Daniel, you sadist, let *go* of me! You're crushing m
to death! If you don't release me this instant, I'll neve
marry you!'

'You mean you *will* marry me?' He released her bu
only partially. 'Donna Kent, *answer* me!'

He was shaking her now and she laughed up at him, teasing him right to the end, though she knew she shouldn't. He had been through enough. Delia had made her realise that. She had been appalled at Donna's saying she was going away for a few weeks, at a loss to understand it. And she'd been right, it had been a stupid idea. Daniel had waited long enough.

'Certainly I'll marry you, provided you take me indoors this very instant!'

With that, she was scooped into Daniel's arms and he carried her to the threshold of the home they had so carefully put together. There, he paused. 'And why are you going to marry me?' he asked, his eyes gentle on hers.

'Because I love you,' she said softly, her heart thumping frantically inside her as she saw the joy on his face. 'Oh, Daniel, I've been such a fool!'

He carried her into the warmth of the drawing room and lowered her on to the white, impractical but gorgeous settee he had spent a small fortune on. He sat beside her, taking both her hands in his. 'I'll thank you not to speak so harshly of my future wife.'

His future wife! Her heart started thumping abnormally again. 'Daniel, about that, about the future——'

'It's going to be beautiful, Donna, every inch of the way. I shall do my utmost to make you happy.'

'And I you,' she smiled. 'I've sold my house in the Wolds and I'm also giving up my business.'

Daniel caught hold of her chin, looking closely into her eyes. 'Are you very sure you want to do that?'

'Absolutely. Totally. I've spoken to Siggy and he's going to keep the pâtisserie on.' She grinned at the memory of her conversation with him. 'He said he thinks he's learned enough from me to keep it profitable now. He suggested I sell the catering side of the business as a going concern but what is there to sell, really? There's no stock to speak of. I'll just let it fizzle out.' She shrugged, she really didn't give a hoot about the business, not now. 'There are a few bookings in the diary and Siggy said he'll do them, but he won't take any more.'

'Darling, I'm delighted, but are you sure? I mean, will I be enough for you? Will it be enough for you, just being my wife?'

'It's all I want.' Her eyes were shining as she looked at him, loving him, wanting him. 'That, and being a mother to your children ... Daniel, I feel it's very important to have this conversation, to talk about the future. I—you would like to have children, wouldn't you?'

'But of course!' He was laughing at her sudden seriousness, but Donna persisted.

'How many?'

'Eh? Well—I haven't really thought about it!'

'Then think about it.'

Daniel had a very good idea what this was all about but he wasn't going to say anything right now. Delia had done a very thorough job, very thorough! He looked at Donna in utmost seriousness, showing not a hint of amusement even in his eyes. 'Ten or twelve would be nice, I suppose.'

Donna started, almost recoiling from him before he threw back his head and roared with laughter. 'Oh, *you*! Daniel! For one awful moment I thought you meant it! Now then, how about ... two or three?' she asked, cuddling close to him.

'Sounds fine by me,' he said softly, nuzzling the side of her neck, sending delicious tingling sensations down the entire length of her body. 'How about starting on the project right now ...?'

Coming Next Month

Available in April wherever paperback books are sold, or through Harlequin Reader Service:

In the U.S.
P.O. Box 1397
Buffalo, N.Y.
14240-1397

In Canada
P.O. Box 2800, Postal Sation A
5170 Yonge Street
Willowdale, Ontario M2N 6J3

Six exciting series for you every month... from Harlequin

Harlequin Romance·
The series that started it all

Tender, captivating and heartwarming...
love stories that sweep you off to faraway places
and delight you with the magic of love.

◆

Harlequin Presents·
Powerful contemporary love stories...as individual as the women who read them

The No. 1 romance series...
exciting love stories for you, the woman of today...
a rare blend of passion and dramatic realism.

◆

Harlequin Superromance®
It's more than romance...
it's Harlequin Superromance

A sophisticated, contemporary romance-fiction
series, providing you with a longer,
more involving read...a richer mix of complex plots,
realism and adventure.

*You're invited to accept
4 books and a
surprise gift Free!*

Acceptance Card

Mail to: **Harlequin Reader Service®**

In the U.S.
901 Fuhrmann Blvd.
P.O. Box 1394
Buffalo, N.Y. 14240-1394

In Canada
P.O. Box 2800, Postal Station A
5170 Yonge Street
Willowdale, Ontario M2N 6J3

YES! Please send me 4 free Harlequin Presents® novels and my free surprise gift. Then send me 8 brand new novels every month as they come off the presses. Bill me at the low price of $1.75 each ($1.95 in Canada)—an 11% saving off the retail price. There are no shipping, handling or other hidden costs. There is no minimum number of books I must purchase. I can always return a shipment and cancel at any time. Even if I never buy another book from Harlequin, the 4 free novels and the surprise gift are mine to keep forever.

108 BPP-BPGE

_____
Name   (PLEASE PRINT)

_____
Address   Apt. No.

_____
City   State/Prov.   Zip/Postal Code

This offer is limited to one order per household and not valid to present subscribers. Price is subject to change.

ACP-SUB-1R

WORLDWIDE LIBRARY IS YOUR TICKET TO ROMANCE, ADVENTURE AND EXCITEMENT

Experience it all in these big, bold Bestsellers— Yours exclusively from WORLDWIDE LIBRARY WHILE QUANTITIES LAST

To receive these Bestsellers, complete the order form, detach and send together with your check or money order (include 75¢ postage and handling), payable to WORLDWIDE LIBRARY, to:

In the U.S.
WORLDWIDE LIBRARY
901 Fuhrmann Blvd.
Buffalo, N.Y. 14269

In Canada
WORLDWIDE LIBRARY
P.O. Box 2800, 5170 Yonge Street
Postal Station A, Willowdale, Ontario
M2N 6J3

Quant.	Title	Price
_____	WILD CONCERTO, Anne Mather	$2.95
_____	A VIOLATION, Charlotte Lamb	$3.50
_____	SECRETS, Sheila Holland	$3.50
_____	SWEET MEMORIES, LaVyrle Spencer	$3.50
_____	FLORA, Anne Weale	$3.50
_____	SUMMER'S AWAKENING, Anne Weale	$3.50
_____	FINGER PRINTS, Barbara Delinsky	$3.50
_____	DREAMWEAVER, Felicia Gallant/Rebecca Flanders	$3.50
_____	EYE OF THE STORM, Maura Seger	$3.50
_____	HIDDEN IN THE FLAME, Anne Mather	$3.50
_____	ECHO OF THUNDER, Maura Seger	$3.95
_____	DREAM OF DARKNESS, Jocelyn Haley	$3.95

	YOUR ORDER TOTAL	$_____
	New York and Arizona residents add appropriate sales tax	$_____
	Postage and Handling	$___.75
	I enclose	$_____

NAME _____

ADDRESS _____ APT.# _____

CITY _____

STATE/PROV. _____ ZIP/POSTAL CODE _____

WW-1-3